Tired of constant scraps with the English, by 1837 the Dutch settlers in South Africa had resolved to trek north into the interior.

Orphaned Laura Conway is living with her Dutch step-mother whom she dearly loves, so it seems natural that she should accompany her and her people on the Great Trek. Paul Venter, leader of their small band of trek-kers, is resolutely opposed to Laura's presence, for he can never forget what the English have done to his people. But how can Laura, the daughter of an English captain, overcome his blind hostility? Especially when she is uncertain if her own feelings for Paul are for an enemy or a friend . . .

The Way of the Wagons

Isobel Stewart

MILLS & BOON LIMITED
London · Sydney · Toronto

First published in Great Britain 1983
by Mills & Boon Limited, 15–16 Brook's Mews,
London W1A 1DR

ISBN 0 263 74274 1

04/0583

Set in 10 on 11½ pt Linotron Times

Photoset by Rowland Phototypesetting Ltd
Bury St Edmunds, Suffolk
Made and printed in Great Britain by
Cox and Wyman Ltd, Reading

CHAPTER
ONE

IT was the silence that woke Laura, the deep, black silence of the African night.

She sat up in the huge feather bed she shared with Aletta, her heart thudding, listening to that silence. It was only then that she realised that before the silence, there had been voices. Men's voices.

It had happened before, in these autumn months of 1837. Many times she had awakened like this, hearing the silence when the voices had ceased. And the next day, there was never any mention made of late-night visitors to the farm.

Laura made up her mind. This time, she was going to find out what was happening.

She slipped out of bed, carefully, silently, but Aletta's blonde head made no movement. The bedroom was in complete darkness, but when she opened the door and looked into the voorkamer, the dull glow of the dying fire was enough to show her an empty room, with only the displaced rest-bench, the chairs moved from their usual places, to show that people had been here.

The big front door was slightly open, and she stood beside it, listening. Now she could hear the voices again—outside, round beside the stables, she thought. The moon was half-hidden by fleeting clouds, but she could see enough to walk out soundlessly on to the stoep, and around to the side of the house. Yes, there they were, a group of men, some already on horseback, some still standing talking. The old man, Oom Jan, her stepmother's father, was talking, and Laura, in the shadow of the huge bougainvillea, tried to move near enough to hear what he was saying. Although he was, as always, speaking in Dutch, she had no problem understanding, for during the last year she had seldom heard her own English tongue.

'I still say that when a man has built a home, and raised a family, there he should stay. There are troubles, it is true, but have there not always been troubles? And —the law is the law. While we live under the English, it is right that we obey their laws.'

'While we live under them, indeed, Oom Jan,' one of the men on horseback returned. 'But is there any need for us to live under them any longer? Surely there is land enough in Africa for all of us?'

'All over the Eastern Cape, and among the Boers near Cape Town, too, there is talk,' another man, a younger one, put in eagerly. 'And the talk is always of trekking.'

There was a silence. They were waiting, Laura knew, for the old man—Oom Jan, Uncle Jan—to speak. She heard him sigh.

'Give me a little time,' he said at last. 'I must talk to my wife, and I must talk to Lisbet. I—will send you a message.'

The men on horseback began to move, and Laura, afraid of being discovered by the old man when he came into the house again, turned to hurry back inside. But as she reached the corner, a man came round, from inside the house, hurrying, and before she could do more than gasp, his hand was on her arm, hard.

'Laura!' he said, astonished, and Laura felt her breath, held in fear, now able to escape.

'Oh, Stephen, you gave me such a fright,' she said, shakily.

The moon was suddenly free of clouds, and by its light she could see Stephen Smit looking down at her.

'You hurt me,' she told him, reproachfully, uncomfortable under the steady gaze of his brown eyes. He released her arm, and she rubbed it, glad not to have to look at him.

But he was not to be put off.

'What are you doing here, Laura?' he asked her.

She thought of saying that she had come out for some fresh air, but the autumn night was chill, and besides, she was certain that under Stephen's direct gaze her voice would stumble.

'I heard voices,' she said, reluctantly. 'I have heard people here before, Stephen, and I wanted to know what was happening. So—so I came out.'

He looked down at her, and Laura was all at once uncomfortably aware that she had not even drawn a kaross around her nightgown. She felt a wave of warm colour rush to her cheeks.

'No shoes, I see,' he said. 'I would have thought you had lived here long enough to remember the danger of scorpions.'

In spite of herself, Laura gave a small gasp, for in her eagerness she had given no thought to the scorpions.

'Stephen,' she whispered, although in the sound of the men riding off there was no need to whisper. 'What is happening? What is it they want Oom Jan to do?'

He shook his head.

'I can say nothing here and now, Laura—any moment Oom Jan will be coming. It is fortunate for you that I went into the house to leave a letter for Tante Martha from my mother. Now go inside, quickly, and for the moment it would be best that you forget anything you have heard tonight.'

Laura shook her head.

'I cannot do that, Stephen,' she said, stubbornly. 'This is no passing thing, I know that by the way those men spoke. And I am no child, I am nineteen years of age.'

In the moonlight, she saw his expression soften.

'And in your nightdress, with your hair braided, you look more like nine years,' he told her. 'Laura—'

'I will go inside,' she said, hastily. 'But—Stephen —will you tell me tomorrow why Oom Jan spoke of leaving his home?'

'Tomorrow I cannot come here,' he told her, 'for I have to ride to Grahamstown in search of the cattle stolen by the Kaffirs. There is some unbelievable story about all the stolen cattle being in the possession of the English, and said to be Government property. The day after, if I am back, I will ride over, Laura, and we can talk. But in the meanwhile—promise me you will be silent.'

Laura heard the old man bid the last of his midnight guests a good night. Now he would come inside, and Stephen was right, he must not find her.

'All right, Stephen,' she agreed. 'But—you must keep your promise, you must tell me what is happening.'

In the shadow of the stoep, he nodded, and Laura —moving carefully now, wishing she had taken the few extra moments to slip her feet into her veldskoens, hurried inside. Aletta murmured in her sleep as Laura slipped in beside her, but fortunately did not wake.

The next morning, as the previous times, there was no mention made of any men coming to see the old farmer. When Laura went through, the voorkamer was already back as it should be, and the big table ready for the family to breakfast.

Laura, eating the mealie porridge and the homemade rusks she had grown accustomed to, found herself unable to keep herself from an occasional glance at the old man at the head of the table. But there was nothing to be read from his face, it was as always—stern, strong, uncompromising and reserved. His wife, Tante Martha, was plump and sweet-faced, and she would seldom, Laura knew, dare to contradict her husband in anything.

Next to Tante Martha sat Lisbet, Laura's stepmother, and the old couple's eldest daughter. Her brown head was bent, as she helped little Dirkie to put milk on his porridge. But when she raised her head, Laura could see that she looked slightly anxious, the way she did all the time now.

She never looked like that in Cape Town, Laura thought mutinously, for she loved the gentle woman who had married her father. Her own mother had died when she was a child, and Lisbet was the only mother she had known.

Beside his mother, Dirkie scuffed at the chairleg, and Laura frowned at him, for he would be in trouble if his grandfather saw him doing anything other than sitting eating his breakfast. Dirkie—from the moment he had been born, this small stepbrother, Laura had loved him completely and unreservedly.

'Sit still, Dirkie,' Aletta said sharply, and colour flooded the small boy's cheeks. He looked anxiously at his grandfather, but for once the old man seemed to have more on his mind than a fidgeting child. But still, Aletta needn't have said anything, Laura thought with resentment. She could have just given Dirkie a nudge, or even a small kick under the table.

Aletta was Lisbet's young sister—there had been other children in between these two, Laura knew, but they had not survived the harsh frontier life. She was a year younger than Laura, and the two girls shared a room and a bed, but the friendship and companionship that Lisbet Smit Conway had hoped for between her step-daughter and her young sister, had not come about.

Laura's eyes and her thoughts—ever prone to wander during the silent meals—went back to her stepmother, and a pang went through her as she saw that there were one or two silver hairs amongst the brown of Lisbet's head. Lisbet was not yet in her mid-thirties, but the silver had come, Laura knew, after John Conway was killed in one of the skirmishes with the Kaffirs on the border.

No, Laura told herself, no, I will not think of my father.

The ache and the longing and the loneliness seemed to her no easier than they had been at the time of his death. Perhaps, she sometimes thought, if Lisbet had chosen to stay in Cape Town, where Laura had friends, where she could speak her own tongue—but Lisbet, broken by her loss, had immediately accepted her father's invitation to come home to the farm in the Eastern Cape. Admittedly, there had been some reservation on the part of her people towards Laura. She had sensed this on the few visits they had made to the farm in the years since Lisbet married her father. They had had to accept their daughter's marriage to an Englishman, and a soldier at that, and the little boy, Dirkie, was of their own blood and so he too was accepted. But Laura herself was a constant reminder of Lisbet's unfortunate marriage to the English Captain.

'I do not wish to be disturbed,' the old man said

suddenly, rising from the table. His fierce grey eyes met Laura's so piercingly that for a moment she was certain that he knew she had been on the stoep the night before, overhearing all that had been said, all that was causing him so much thought and concern. But he said nothing more, and she knew that she had imagined it.

But she did not imagine that everyone was strange, tense and waiting, through the next two days. The old people—Lisbet—Aletta. Aletta, Laura knew, was annoyed because Stephen Smit did not come, and she took her annoyance out on Laura, for she resented, Laura could see, that the younger girl knew Stephen had ridden to Grahamstown and she did not. Laura herself wished she had kept silent about mentioning where the young farmer was, but the damage was done.

'When did he tell you?' Aletta asked suspiciously.

Laura, remembering the unplanned meeting on the stoep in the moonlight, pretended that she did not remember when Stephen had told her, but this only made matters worse.

'It seems very strange to me,' Aletta said, 'that Stephen should talk of going to Grahamstown to you, and not to his own cousin.'

'Second cousin,' Laura reminded her levelly, but the comment, far from annoying Aletta, pleased her, and Laura knew all too well why. The relationship was close enough, but at the same time not too close. From the time she came here to the farm, Aletta had made it all too clear that she regarded Stephen as her own property. But Stephen, Laura had begun more and more to realise, thought differently.

The next day, late in the afternoon, he came. He kissed old Mrs Smit, whom he called by the courtesy title of Tante Martha, and he kissed Lisbet and Aletta, and he greeted Laura and Dirkie. But the line of his jaw was grim, set, and his dark eyes were sombre Laura saw with dismay.

'I am sorry Oom Jan is out,' he said, tightly, 'for I have much to say to him. No, Tante, it must wait. He will be back at sundown, you say?'

The old woman nodded.

'You will stay and eat with us, nephew,' she invited him. 'Then you can talk to him.'

How can she be so placid, Laura thought, her own emotions torn by the way Stephen looked. But then, for a moment, as Stephen went out of the voorkamer, she saw the way the old woman's eyes rested on him, troubled and concerned, and she was ashamed of her impatience.

She and Aletta were supposed to be sewing, helping Lisbet to mend the linen, but Laura at the first opportunity slipped out, determined to find Stephen, to ask him what had happened.

At the back door, she hesitated, uncertain where he might be.

'Laura,' her stepmother said from the kitchen, and Laura swung round guiltily.

But Lisbet only held out Laura's sunbonnet, so often the cause of argument between them. Laura contented herself with a heavy sigh as she took the sunbonnet and tied it on.

'You say you do not mind these freckles now, but the day may come when you do,' Lisbet said, smiling, and she turned and went inside.

There was an old mirror near the back door, and Laura looked into it, setting her sunbonnet straight. Her mouth—wider than beauty or fashion decreed—was still somewhat mutinous, and there were tendrils of soft brown hair escaping from the sunbonnet. Impatiently, Laura pushed them out of the way. Untidy hair—a dusting of freckles on her nose—no wonder she was often the despair of her stepmother. Unwillingly, the grey eyes of the girl in the mirror softened in a smile, as she turned away. But what do I care of wide mouths, or of freckles, she thought, when there is so much disturbance around?

She found Stephen in the stable, supervising the Hottentot servant who was rubbing down his horse.

'Stephen,' she said, softly.

He looked down at her, his eyes still bleak.

'Did you find your stolen cattle?' she asked him.

He laughed, a laugh with no mirth in it, and this was so unlike the good-tempered Stephen, that Laura knew there was something far wrong.

'Yes, we found them,' he told her. 'And the story was right. They are safe in the kraal in Grahamstown—and they are Government property. If we choose to, we can go along to the next market and bid for them. Bid for them—our own cattle, stolen from us by the Kaffirs!'

He patted the horse's neck, and then, when he turned back to Laura, some of the bleakness had left his eyes.

'Come, let us walk down by the dam, and I will tell you what you want to know,' he said, abruptly.

Laura, eager as she was to ask him questions, knew that she was better to remain silent, to wait for him to speak. And at last, beside the dam, he began.

'It is difficult for you, being English, to understand, Laura,' he said, slowly. 'But my people are seething now with grievances and injustices like this. And I think the others are right. The time has come to act.'

'I—would like to understand, Stephen,' Laura said,

uncertainly. 'I know that there was much talk about the compensation for freeing the slaves.'

'One injustice among many,' Stephen replied. 'Oh, Laura, there have been so many over the years. I do not concern myself with things that happened twenty years ago, because there is enough and to spare today. And the outcome of it all is that the people are determined to move away from the rule of the English, to trek with all that they possess, until they find a place where they can live in peace, in the way they choose.'

Laura looked up at him, this tall and usually gentle young man she had known now for over a year.

'And you, Stephen?' she asked him. 'How do you feel?'

His eyes were on the far horizons.

'I look on Oom Jan as the head of our family, with my own father dead, and I will abide by his decision,' he said, quietly. 'But—I hope that what I have to tell him today will help him to make that decision.' He turned, and smiled, with difficulty. 'But these are serious things to be talking of, Laura, and there are many other things I would rather discuss, for it is not often that I am fortunate enough to have a little time with you alone. Laura—'

What Stephen would have said, she was not to know, for at that moment, Aletta came through the trees, her face flushed, her golden hair escaping its pins.

'I thought you might be here,' she said to Laura coolly. And then, to Stephen, 'My grandfather is home, and he wishes to see you, Stephen.' She looked down, her lashes dark on the cream of her skin. 'I think you had better hurry, for he seems impatient.'

For a moment, Stephen's eyes held Laura's, and Laura, confused, uncertain, knew that the moment was only deferred, that Stephen would later speak of what he had wanted to. Then, without a word, he turned and walked swiftly back towards the farmhouse.

Laura began to walk back as well, but she was not to be let off as lightly. Aletta caught up with her, and Laura's heart sank at the hostility in the other girl's face.

'You need not imagine that this is anything more than a passing fancy for Stephen,' she said abruptly. 'His family and my family decided long ago that he and I would marry.' Now her confidence faltered. 'So—so if he has asked you to promise yourself to him, it means nothing.'

'That is up to Stephen, I think,' Laura replied, as composedly as she could. 'In any case, he has not asked me. We are friends, he and I. We like to talk to each other.'

'All you want is to keep him ensnared,' Aletta said, and the fury in her voice made Laura laugh.

'Aletta,' she said, and she put her hand on the other girl's arm, 'let us not quarrel, and let us not have words like ensnare. I am far from being a femme fatale, you know. And besides, you have made yourself so angry, your sunbonnet is off, and your beautiful skin will burn. You might even cause freckles like mine, and no amount of buttermilk will take them away, you know!'

Aletta snatched her arm away, but in spite of her anger, she took a minute to tie her sunbonnet firmly over her golden head again.

'You are impossible,' she said, furiously. 'You just laugh at me!'

She lifted her skirts, then, and ran the rest of the way. Laura, watching her, felt the smile on her lips fade. I laugh, Aletta, she thought, forlornly, because sometimes, if I don't, I might weep. And my father would not want me to weep.

She lifted her chin, resolutely, and went the rest of the way back to the house alone.

For the rest of the day, that was how she felt. Very much alone. The old man and Stephen sat together in the voorkamer for much of the time talking, Stephen's brown head close to the old man's snowy one. Sometimes Tante Martha was with them, sometimes Lisbet. Then, as soon as it was dark, Stephen rode off, without saying goodbye. When Dirkie had been put to bed, Oom Jan turned to Laura and Aletta.

'You are not to retire yet, *meisies*,' he said. 'Stephen has gone to fetch some of our neighbours, and we are to have a meeting. I wish you both to be here, for you are no longer children.'

He would say nothing more, but retired to his favourite corner, on the rest-bench, with the big family bible open on his knee. But Laura, watching him, saw that although his eye rested on the page, he was not reading. And although she had never been able to come close to him, she felt all at once pity for him, with such a decision to make.

For the first time, then, sitting waiting in the voorkamer, she could no longer keep at bay the anxiety of what was to become of her if Oom Jan decided to trek. Although she had often, in the last year, been conscious that she was not entirely welcome here among the Boers of the Eastern Cape, because she loved Lisbet, and Dirkie, she had come to regard it as her home. And—if they went, what of a girl who had no real claim on them at all?

When her father died, there had been a letter from an aunt in England, the only relative, it seemed, prepared to give her dead brother's daughter a home. But the letter was stiff, so lacking any real feeling, that Laura, heartbroken and bewildered, had been only too glad to accept Lisbet's decision that she was to remain with them. Now—

The huge front door opened, and Stephen came in, a group of neighbouring farmers with him. Laura recognised some of the men she had seen dimly the other night, outside the stables. They greeted Tante Martha, and the old man, and Lisbet, but there was obviously no time to be wasted on unnecessary pleasantries, and when they had nodded to the two girls, they sat down, their eyes on Oom Jan.

'You have decided, Oom Jan?' one of the men asked, but the old man was not to be rushed.

'I have thought much about this matter,' he said, ponderously, 'and I have read much in the Book. Today, when Stephen told me of what had happened in Grahamstown, I knew the time had come. I am certain that it is the Lord's will that we trek.'

The younger among the men could barely restrain their pleasure at his decision, but one of the older farmers said, nodding seriously, 'It is the right decision, Jan, of that I am certain. Many among our people have come to this decision. There is Pieter Retief of the Winterberg, and Gerrit Maritz of Graaff-Reinet—solid, good-thinking men. They too will trek.' He looked around him. 'And now, we have plans to make, my friends. We must decide how many wagons we take, we must reckon the number of animals. We will be a good size of trek, big enough for protection, but not yet over-large. Now, let us start reckoning.'

'Just a minute, Jan,' another man said, and Laura, shaken, saw his cold grey eyes were on her. 'There is another matter to be decided first. What of the English girl?'

It seemed to Laura that every person in the room was looking at her. She wanted to speak, to lift her head proudly and tell them that she could look after herself, that she had no need of anything from them. But her throat was tight, aching with hurt at the rejection she saw on so many faces. And so she sat, silent.

'We have enough to worry about with our own people,' another grey-haired farmer muttered. 'I see no reason why—'

Then, before he could say any more, Lisbet Smit Conway had crossed the room, and her arms were warm and firm around Laura.

'I will give you good reason,' she said, and her voice was high and clear. 'Laura's father was my husband, and Laura is as dear to me as my own child.'

She looked around them all, and her arm tightened around Laura.

'If you do not wish Laura to trek with us,' she said, 'then I will not trek either!'

CHAPTER
TWO

BEFORE Laura's stepmother had finished speaking, Stephen was there too, at Laura's other side.

'And I say the same,' he said, levelly. 'If you are not prepared to take Laura with us, then I do not go either.'

Laura, at last able to speak, turned to him.

'Oh, Stephen,' she said, shakily, 'there is no need for you to do that. And—they are your people, Mother—of course you must go.'

Across the room, there was a murmur of voices, and a movement as men, old and young, talked amongst themselves. Then, before any of them could speak out, Oom Jan stood up.

'There will be no further talk of that kind,' he said, sternly. 'My daughter has taken responsibility for this girl, and that is good enough for me. Laura treks with us.'

'Of course, of course, Oom Jan,' one of the men said hastily. 'We were only getting the matter clear.'

Tante Martha lifted her white head, and her sweet, lined face was stern.

'The "English girl", indeed,' she said severely. 'Laura is an orphan who has been welcomed into our family. It is as my husband says. She treks with us.'

Laura looked from the old woman to the old man wonderingly, her throat tight at this unexpected support.

'Thank you,' she murmured, not quite steadily. 'Thank you, Tante Martha—Oom Jan.'

But the support, she saw, stopped at Aletta, whose blue eyes were cool and hostile, and Laura knew, with complete certainty, that she would have been only too pleased if Laura had been left behind.

In the days that followed, there was much to do, now that the decision to trek had been made. There was stock to be sold, for valuable as the sheep and the cattle would be to them in the new life, there was a limit to what could be taken. Stephen was sent to Grahamstown to sell half of Oom Jan's stock, as well as half of his own. And while he was gone, the women of the household busied themselves with mending linen that was to be taken.

Laura hated this, for her fingers had always been clumsy with a needle, and she begrudged the hours spent sitting on the rest-bench working, when she might have been wandering over the farm, storing in her heart the places that had become dearer to her than she had realised in the year she had lived here. Instead of sitting here, she thought mutinously, as she pricked her finger once more, she could have been walking up beside the dam, watching the birds that made their nests on its shore, pointing them out to Dirkie. Or she could have been out riding over the veld, her hair flying, disregarding Lisbet's warnings of her skin freckling in the sunlight, or her admonitions on how unladylike she was.

But as she sat beside Lisbet, in the cool of the voorkamer, with the little boy playing at their feet, she knew that it would have broken her heart if she had had to part from these two people. For although she might rebel at times against Lisbet's gentle rebukes, she knew that it was done because her stepmother loved her, because she believed it was for the best that Laura should be more

although Dirkie was too young to understand. It was the idea that appealed to him—the living in wagons, the moving on every day. Aletta, echoing Stephen, spoke of the wide frontiers, of the places where the Boers could live in peace, away from the rule of the English. Each time she did this, Laura refused to respond, forcing herself to say nothing. But as the days of preparation reached their climax, she thought more and more often how strange it was that she, an English girl, should be content to leave the last contact with her own people, and go off on this trek.

And yet, she thought now, in the darkness of the empty house, I have no people of my own, other than Lisbet and Dirkie. And so, where they go, I must go too. Somehow, there was peace in that thought, an acceptance of what she was about to do. The alternative—to go to her father's sister in England, to cut her ties with Lisbet and Dirkie, never to see them again—was unthinkable.

She wandered out on to the stoep, and she thought of that night she had bumped into Stephen here. If I could have allowed him to speak when he kissed me, it would have been different, she thought. He is right in that—my position would have had no problems then. But—

But what, she wondered, as she sometimes had, since the day she had stopped him from speaking. Stephen was good and kind, he was agreeable to look at, he was a young man of substance, with what he had inherited from his father, and she certainly had not minded when he kissed her. Just as she had not minded when the young officers had kissed her.

But there must be more than that, Laura thought now, the darkness and the loneliness giving clarity to the confusion of her feelings. She leaned against the cool thick wall of the house, her eyes closed. Somewhere, she thought, somewhere there is a man who will turn my blood to fire, and my limbs to water, a man who will take me in his arms with passion as well as with tenderness, a man—

Warm colour flooded her cheeks at the shamelessness of her thoughts. She would go back to the wagon, she decided, whether or not she could sleep. But as she went back down the steps, she saw the wavering light of a candle go past the stoep and on towards the back of the house.

Tante Martha, she thought, surprised, for the old woman had seemed to be asleep when she crept from the wagon. Perhaps she was ill. She followed the candle, concerned, and it was only as she caught up with Tante Martha, that she realised where she was going. The tiny graveyard, where three of her children lay.

Laura wanted to turn back, but it was too late, the old woman had heard her.

'I'm sorry, Tante,' Laura said, awkwardly. 'I thought you were ill, I did not think that of course this is where you would be coming.'

She could see, by the dim candlelight, that the old woman's eyes were wet.

'I came to say my goodbyes, my child,' she said, simply. 'It is sadder for me to leave this small piece of ground than to leave my house. When I am gone, no one will come here, no one will remember my Margriet, my Paul, my Jannie.' She turned away, and Laura's own eyes blurred as she saw how carefully, how lovingly, the old woman shut the small gate. Unaccountably, a desolation swept over her as she thought of the years to come, and the big solid house sitting here, neglected, empty, the wind sweeping through the swinging doors, the broken windows. And the gate of this little graveyard swinging, broken and forgotten. Then, through the desolation, she felt the old woman's hand on her arm, warm and reassuring. 'Now I have said goodbye, and my duty is to the living. Give me your arm, Laura, for the path is uneven. You have known your losses too, child. I think you understand. But you are young, and it is tomorrow you must think of, not yesterday—that is only permitted for an old woman like me. Now I am done with yesterday—tomorrow we trek.'

The wagons rolled away from the deserted farm at dawn, and Laura saw that there were few who looked back. All of them, young and old alike, were determined now to look ahead.

Within a few days, it seemed to Laura that she had never known any other life but this, so quickly did the rhythm and the pattern of the trekking days become accepted. There was the early rise, and the bustle as the oxen were inspanned and the coffee was made. Then the hours of sitting inside the wagon or on the seat at the front, or sometimes sitting at the back, her bare feet swinging—although Aletta refused to do this, saying it was not seemly. Laura envied the men, riding off into the bush at the side of the swaying wagons, or riding ahead to plan the route.

At night, they would outspan and encamp in clearings trampled by treks before them, the fires would be lit, the cooking-pots would come out, and the women would come into their own. Sometimes, through the day, they would see in the distance, ahead of them or behind them, the wagons of another trek.

It would take them, Stephen and the other men reckoned, almost three weeks to reach Graaff-Reinet, and this they were eager to do, for they wanted news of Pieter Retief, whose trek they hoped to join.

One week away from Graaff-Reinet, Laura sat on the back of the wagon one afternoon, her bare feet, sunburned now, swinging. Off in the veld she could see horsemen, and she wondered, idly, if the men from the trek had found plenty of game to shoot for tonight's meal. Then one of the horsemen galloped closer, and she saw that it was no one from their own trek. He reined in just a little ahead of her to speak to Oom Jan, Laura shaded her eyes against the sun, and looked at him.

Afterwards, she was to remember so clearly that first time she saw Paul Venter. One hand on the reins of his horse, the other pushing his hat back on his thick fair hair. He was a big man, and she could see the muscles rippling under his shirt. His eyes were very blue in the brown of his face.

She had not heard what he said, but just as he finished, he caught sight of her. He smiled, his eyes on her bare brown feet, and swept his hat off before turning and riding away. A tide of colour warmed Laura's cheeks, and she got back inside the wagon.

'Who was that?' she asked the old man, casually.

'His name is Paul Venter,' Oom Jan told her. 'He is the leader of a small trek, and he would like to trek with us, I have said we will talk tonight.'

That night, when they had stopped, the men gathered under a tree to talk, while the women prepared the evening meal. Laura, catching sight of a tall blond head, taller than any other man there, longed to hear what was being said, but of course she could not go any nearer. In any case, her stepmother had asked her to keep an eye on Dirkie, active and full of mischief after being confined for the day. Now, he was playing with some of the other small boys, and they ran across the clearing. Laura gathered up her skirts and ran after them, but before she reached them, Dirkie had climbed into the spreading branches of a tree.

'Come down, Dirkie,' she told him, grabbing another small boy before he could follow.

Dirkie shook his head.

'Mother will be very angry if you tear your trousers,' she told him severely. 'Come down this minute.'

The child shook his head again, but now there was a quiver in his lip.

'I don't think I can, Laura,' he said, a little shakily.

'Of course you can,' Laura told him, her voice brisk to try and hide the sinking in her heart. 'If you got up, you can get down.'

'I can't,' Dirkie said flatly.

Laura looked up at him. All he had to do was get over to that big branch again, and he could get down easily. But he did look small, up there.

She sighed, hitched up her skirt, and began to climb. With her longer reach, it wasn't difficult, and when she reached Dirkie, the warmth and the tightness of his arms around her, made it worthwhile. Carefully, she lowered him on to the big branch, and watched him make his way down.

She was never sure what happened after that. Perhaps her skirt caught in a branch, perhaps she lost her footing. But with no warning, she felt herself falling, and her head banged against the trunk of the tree so hard that she knew nothing more until she found herself lying there, hearing Dirkie sobbing, and saying her name.

'She's dead—Laura's dead,' he sobbed.

Laura wanted to tell him that she wasn't dead, but stunned as she was, she could get no words out. I've got to move, she thought, dazed. But the next moment she heard a strange voice tell Dirkie, with authority, to stand back, and then she was swung, gently but firmly, into strong arms. Once again, she tried to speak, but no more than a murmur would come.

'Lie still,' the voice told her.

Laura opened her eyes, knowing even before she did so, who was holding her. His arms were strong and confident as he strode across the clearing carrying her, and her head lay against his chest. I can feel his heart beating, she thought, confusedly.

Somehow, Paul Venter managed to climb into the wagon with her still in his arms, and he laid her down on her bed, gently. Laura, her eyes closed, heard Dirkie crying now, telling his mother what had happened.

'No, she isn't dead, my boy,' the big stranger said, and she could hear laughter in his voice. 'I could feel her heart beating—she's only stunned. She didn't fall very far.'

For some reason Laura, even in her stunned state, and with an ache beginning in her head, found it a most disturbing thought—that he had been conscious of her heart beating, just as she had been conscious of his.

Then, before she could make another attempt to open her eyes, to thank him, she heard him brush aside Lisbet's thanks, and take his leave. Then Lisbet was kneeling beside her, her hand cool on Laura's head.

'You shouldn't have climbed up after Dirkie,' she told Laura shakily. 'You should have got one of the men.'

Then she bathed Laura's aching head, and told her she was to stay in bed. By that time, the ache in Laura's head stopped her from arguing, and she was glad to lie there quietly in the wagon, sleeping a little, waking to eat a little gruel, and then sleeping again. The next day, apart from an ache in her head and some stiffness in her limbs, she felt much better. She looked for Paul Venter, to thank him, but he had ridden ahead with some of the other men.

In the evening, Laura thought often throughout that day, I will thank him. It would be most impolite if I did not do that. After all, he lifted me up, and he carried me across to the wagon, and he laid me down on my bed. Yes, when we encamp tonight the first thing I must do is find him and thank him.

Dirkie was forbidden to wander away from his mother when they camped that night, and Laura was told she need not help with the food, she was just to walk around a little. But gently, Lisbet told her.

Paul Venter was beside his wagon, he had just finished setting his oxen free. His back was towards her, and he straightened up just as she reached him. He was even bigger than she had thought, Laura realised.

She touched his arm.

'Mr Venter,' she said, surprised to find that her voice was not quite steady. 'I—I wanted to thank you for looking after me yesterday.'

He turned and looked down at her, unsmiling.

'It—it was very kind of you,' Laura said, taken aback by the coolness of his clear blue eyes, those same blue eyes that had smiled only yesterday at the sight of her bare feet at the back of the wagon.

'I want no thanks from you, Miss Conway,' he said, coolly. 'I had no idea when we joined this trek, that we were to be with the daughter of an English soldier!' He bowed.

And Laura, dismayed and shaken, watched him walk away from her, without looking back.

CHAPTER
THREE

In that moment of hurt and humiliation, all Laura wanted to do was run into the shelter of the trees, away from the amused glances of the people around who had seen how Paul Venter had spoken to her.

And then, watching the tall figure stride away, she thought with rising anger, No, Mr Paul Venter, no, I will not be spoken to like that!

Without giving herself time to think, she ran after him and put one hand on his arm. He stopped, and looked down at her, obviously taken aback.

'Mr Venter,' Laura said, and she wished she could have stopped her voice from shaking. 'Mr Venter, I would have you know that I am proud to be my father's daughter. He—he was an officer and a gentleman.'

For a moment, something between amusement and —could it be respect?—flickered in the big fair-haired man's blue eyes.

'Neither of which I am, of course, Miss Conway, I take you to mean,' he returned. 'And you are right—I am a simple Boer.'

Laura ignored that.

Raising her chin, she looked up at him.

'He certainly would not have talked to a lady as you did, Mr Venter,' she said coolly, and she was fiercely glad that now she had her voice under control.

Once again Paul Venter bowed.

'I take your point, Miss Conway, and I have no intention of insulting your father's memory. But—' There was nothing now but an icy coolness in his clear blue eyes. 'But I reserve my right to choose my company, and if I had known, then—'

'Then you would not have chosen mine,' Laura finished for him, furiously. 'That suits me very well, Mr Venter, for I certainly would not choose to be in your company!'

And this time, she had the satisfaction of being the one who turned and walked away.

In the wagon, she sat down, grateful for the darkness to hide the scarlet of her cheeks, grateful that Tante Martha and Lisbet were both busy out at the cooking fires, making the evening meal. But a moment later Aletta appeared in the doorway, and even in the dim light Laura could tell that the other girl had seen what had happened between her and Paul Venter.

'Well, well,' Aletta said, mockingly, 'it must be a change for you, Laura, to have a man show so clearly that he is not interested in you, and a man as good-looking as Paul Venter, at that!'

'I do not find him good-looking in the least,' Laura replied, coolly and untruthfully. And then, without realising until too late that she was contradicting herself —'And even if he is, I find his lack of social graces quite revolting!'

She liked the phrase, and wished she had thought of it in time to say it to Paul Venter himself. But at least she could give herself the satisfaction of repeating it to Stephen, when he came to her early the next morning, as she stood beside the fire drinking hot coffee and eating rusks.

'But what happened?' Stephen said again. 'I came

back late from hunting to find talk through the whole camp of a—a difference of opinion between you and Paul Venter, and now you say you find his lack of social graces revolting. Laura, I insist on knowing what happened.'

Laura looked up at him, saying nothing. After a moment, he coloured, and turned away.

'I beg your pardon,' he said, quietly. 'I have no right to insist. But—if he has insulted you, Laura, then I am not prepared to leave it there. Since you will give me no other grounds, then I claim the right of kinship with your stepmother, for you have no other man to act on your behalf, other than Oom Jan.'

Suddenly, in the early morning light, Laura was conscious of a tall figure near them—near enough to overhear. She could not see Paul Venter's face, but she was certain there would be amusement in it.

'There was no question of insult, Stephen,' she told him. 'Really, it is not worth bothering about. It was as you said, a difference of opinion.'

And then, on an impulse that she did not care to examine too closely, but an impulse that had a great deal to do with Paul Venter standing nearby, she stood on tiptoe and kissed Stephen's cheek.

'But thank you, Stephen,' she said, softly. 'Thank you for—caring about me.'

'Laura,' he began, unsteadily, but she was wishing now that she had not obeyed the impulse, and she drew her hands away from his when he would have caught them and held them.

It had not only been Paul Venter who had been near, she found later, when Aletta's rudeness and hostility made it all too obvious. Quite apart from various barbed remarks that ended in Tanta Martha telling her daughter, with unusual sharpness, to be silent if she could not speak civilly.

'It's all right, Tante Martha,' Laura said, uncomfortably, as Aletta, taking advantage of a momentary pause in the steady roll of the wagon, climbed down and went to sit in the wagon behind, with her friend Sara.

The old woman sighed.

'Perhaps we have spoiled her,' she said, her voice heavy. 'But there were the three who died, after Lisbet, and we thought there would be no more. Then she came to us, in the autumn of our lives, our *laatlammetjie*, our little late lamb, and we were so happy to have her, Laura, that perhaps it was easy to let her have her own way. But—I am sorry she does not behave like a sister to you, for that is what Lisbet and I had hoped, that the two of you would be company for each other, that you would grow close.'

Laura looked at her stepmother, knowing all too well that this was what Lisbet had hoped. All at once she was ashamed of herself.

'I will try harder,' she said, her voice low. But even as she said it she knew that it would be of little use, while Stephen continued to look at her as he had never looked at Aletta.

Day after day, the wagons rolled steadily towards the mountains, heading for Graaff-Reinet. The trekkers rose early, ready to start at dawn, to cover as much ground as possible before the heat of the day. Sometimes when they stopped at night, they met other small groups of trekkers, and occasionally these small groups would decide to join the larger trek, and would talk to Oom Jan and the other leaders. Laura could not help noticing that already Paul Venter had become a man whose opinion was valued, whose thoughts were sought when any decision had to be made. Often Laura would see his tall blond head, hat pushed well back on the thick fair hair, in the middle of the group of men. But any time she came near him when they were encamped, she turned away, so that they would not meet, so that he would not have any further opportunity to reject and humiliate her.

Suddenly the mountains which had been so distant, were near, and they were in the foothills, the wagons being laboriously pulled up by the oxen. There was no road, only a series of narrow ledges, with massive boulders often making the way impassable. Oom Jan and Stephen were forced to ask the younger women to dismount and make their own way up, to lighten the burden on the team of oxen. Laura, seeing the way the wagon heaved and blundered its way upwards, was only too glad to be on foot, and she wondered how Tante Martha fared, sitting inside.

'Careful, Dirkie,' Lisbet said, as the small boy stepped close to the narrow and precipitous ledge.

'It's a long way down, Dirkie,' Laura told her small brother, and she grasped his hand firmly. 'Now come back and stay beside Mother and I.'

This had been the easiest way through the mountains, for the pathfinders had spent days ranging ahead, trying to find the least difficult and dangerous way for the wagons. Other wagons had come this way before them, they could see the ruts embedded deep in the rock. But Laura marvelled at how they had done it.

There was a shout ahead of them and Dirkie evaded her hand and ran ahead of the wagon. Laura followed him, knowing that every moment he was out of his mother's sight would cause Lisbet concern. She caught him just as he clambered on top of a huge boulder.

'What has happened, Dirkie?' she asked him, breathless after the climb.

'It's the Nels' wagon,' he told her, between excitement and alarm. 'Laura, the first two oxen have slipped over the edge, and now the wagon's almost falling.'

Her heart in her mouth, Laura forgot propriety, hitched up her skirts, and climbed up beside him, her arm around him. He was right, the two leading oxen had lost their footing and now hung over the edge, held only by the trek-tow. And behind them, the wagon itself seemed to be moving closer to the edge, as the rest of the team of oxen, in their panic, edged forward. There were screams from the wagon and Laura, chilled, remembered Anna Nel, soon to have a child.

And then, as she watched, Paul Venter was there. His hands grasped the rope firmly, and as the screams from the wagon grew silent, she heard him talk to the team of oxen, steadily, soothingly. All the time he braced himself against the weight of the two beasts already over.

'Cut them loose,' she heard him say, and then, when the men beside him would have argued—'Cut them loose, or you stand to lose the whole team, and the wagon as well. I will hold the team back as well as I can, but you must be quick.'

'Laura,' Dirkie said, shakily, 'are they going to—to let the poor oxen fall over?'

Her arm tightened around him.

'They have to, Dirkie,' she told him. 'But you don't have to look.'

There was a moment of silence, and she heard the small boy draw in his breath.

'Yes, I do have to,' he told her firmly. 'Because —because our father was a soldier, wasn't he, Laura, and soldiers are brave.'

There was an ache of love and grief in Laura's throat. 'Yes, Dirkie, soldiers are brave,' she told him.

She forced herself not to look away, as Stephen Smit joined Paul Venter beside the wagon on the brink of the precipice. There was room for only one man, and Laura wondered how long Paul Venter could take the weight alone, as Stephen and another man began to cut the rope loose. She never knew how long it took, whether it was minutes or hours before the bodies of the two oxen crashed down into the abyss, but her arm around Dirkie was stiff, and his small face was white when at last they climbed down from the huge boulder and went back to their own wagon.

And if it can happen to one wagon, it can happen to another, Laura thought, trying to still the rush of fear, as she told Tante Martha and Lisbet what had happened.

After that, each team of oxen was led by a man, and a strong man at that, sometimes walking backwards, easing and persuading the excited and nervous animals up the steep slopes. But there was no possibility of the trek getting through the pass before nightfall. In fact, it was not even sunset when any further progress became impossible, as streaks of mist appeared around them, a few at first, so that there were momentary and tantalising glimpses of the valley way beneath them. Then, suddenly, the mist thickened, and they were enclosed in its milky whiteness. It was so thick that there was no telling where the brink of the precipice was.

Oom Jan, with a shouted command, held his team of oxen steady. Inside the wagon, Tante Martha was silent, and behind it, Laura and Lisbet looked at each other, the mist swirling around them. And then, through the mist, Paul Venter appeared from ahead. They heard him talk to Oom Jan, and then he was beside them, moving carefully.

'We can go no further tonight,' he said to them. 'We dare not even unyoke or loosen the oxen. I will help Oom Jan to put stones to keep the wagon steady, and after that—there is nothing we can do but wait for morning.'

'What about the other wagons?' Laura asked, unwilling to ask this man anything, yet wanting to know. 'Is everyone else all right?'

He looked down at her, but she thought that he did not perhaps fully realise that it was the English Captain's daughter he was talking to, for there was no hostility in his voice.

'There is no damage,' he said after a moment's hesitation. 'But one wagon will need a wheel repaired when daylight comes.'

'What about the oxen?' Laura asked him. 'They need water, they have worked hard all day.'

'I am afraid they must go thirsty,' he replied, but although the words were unfeeling, she had the strange, disturbing thought that he did not like having to leave the poor beasts unwatered. 'As for you ladies—I am afraid there is no question of preparing any food, we dare not risk anyone moving. The men are coming down the line of wagons, lighting fires. Until they reach you, I must ask you to remain perfectly still.'

Some time later Stephen and some of the other men came and lit a small fire at the back of the wagon. Dirkie, exhausted, was lifted into the wagon beside his grandmother, and Aletta climbed in as well. But all through that long, anxious night, Laura, with her stepmother beside her, sat at the small fire, waiting for morning.

And when it came, it was clear and brilliant, with an

unclouded sky. Suddenly the cold and the misery of the night were forgotten, and the terrors of the mountain pass seemed as if they could be surmounted. They found that they were nearer the top than they had dared to hope, and a few hours took them over, and looking down on the plains of the Great Karroo. Ahead of them, they knew, lay Graaff-Reinet, and the chance to join up with other bands of trekkers, the chance to hear news of possible settling places further into the interior. Somehow even the oxen seemed to pull with a better will, thirsty as they were, and the crisp air brought a feeling of alertness and anticipation to the whole trek.

By night, they had reached the low foothills on the other side of the pass, and the following day the journey across the vast plain began. Laura had begun to teach Dirkie his letters, for there was no teacher, no minister or predikant who might have taken on the responsibility for the teaching of the children. Each day, when they stopped at midday, she would take out his books and work with him for a little while, trying to guide his hand, still chubby, still the hand of a child rather than a boy, to form the letters of the alphabet. That first day on the plain, another two children, from the wagons nearby, came and sat beside her, listening quietly. The older child, a girl of perhaps eight, could already read, although not well, and Laura helped her, and encouraged her, while her brother and Dirkie watched and listened with some envy.

The next day, the children appeared as soon as Laura and Dirkie sat down for their lesson, and after a little while their mother, a baby in her arms, came over to listen to the reading lesson.

'May they come to you tomorrow as well?' she asked, a little shyly, when the books were put away. 'It was worrying me, that they would have no schooling while we trekked.'

In spite of her shyness, she was friendly, and Laura realised, not for the first time, how much she had missed any gestures of real warmth and friendship from anyone other than Lisbet and the old people, and Stephen.

'If you think they would like to, they are welcome,' she replied. 'But I am no teacher, I am just trying to teach Dirkie his letters.'

'And arithmetic?' the young Boer woman asked eagerly. 'Could you not teach them their numbers?'

Laura smiled.

'I can try,' she agreed.

Within a few days, there were six children coming to her little 'school'. In truth, Laura was glad to do this, for it seemed that this was one way she could make herself useful on the trek. She was not needed for the cooking in the evenings, and when there was any sewing or mending to be done, she had to admit that she was of little use. But this, now, was something that she seemed to have a gift for, and she found herself looking forward with some eagerness, each day, to lesson-time.

Her little group of pupils attracted a fair bit of attention, she found. Once or twice, she looked up to find Paul Venter close by, his hat tipped back on his thick fair hair, his lean, brown face still and somehow watchful. And there was another man—she did not know his name, but he had joined their trek a little after Paul Venter's party. More and more often she would become conscious, as she sat on the ground in the shade of the wagon, with the children gathered around her, that she was being watched, and she would find him standing there. He was, she thought, a little older than Paul Venter, perhaps in his late twenties, not a tall man.

There was something in the steady gaze of his grey eyes that made her uncomfortable.

With Graaff-Reinet only a day or so ahead, they encamped one night beside a river. The day had been hot, and the trail dusty, and Laura, as she helped Lisbet and Tante Martha and Aletta to arrange the food and the cooking-pot, could hear the river, the splash of the water on the stones.

If I could only, she thought longingly, put my feet into the coolness of that running water. Once the thought was there, there was no dismissing it, and as soon as it was possible she slipped away, through the trees that grew on the riverbank, round a bend, and out of sight of the camp.

She slipped her feet out of her veldskoene, and they were as dusty as she had thought. But the water was cool, and the dust disappeared from her bare brown feet, as she wriggled her toes with pleasure. I could wash, she thought, if I was just to slip my dress off. Aletta would have been horrified, preferring to make do with a basin of water in the wagon, but Laura longed to feel clean and cool.

Without giving herself time to hesitate, she slipped her dress off, laid it on the riverbank, and then, with her petticoat and her drawers hitched high, and her arms and throat bare above her bodice, she stepped into the water. It was only when she had washed her arms, and the water was trickling deliciously down her back, that a sound from the riverbank made her turn.

He was standing there, watching her, the dark man with the hot grey eyes. And she thought, as her heart hammered against her ribs in instinctive fear, that he had been watching her for some time.

'Well, well,' he said slowly, his eyes never leaving her, 'so school is out early today!'

Laura stepped out of the water, but he moved, deliberately, to stand between her and her dress.

'Please give me my dress,' she said, her head high, determined not to let him see that she was afraid.

He stepped towards her. She would have turned and run, even without her dress, but the pebbles on the river-bank were hard, and she stumbled. The next moment he was there, his arms around her, his lips seeking hers.

Laura, frozen with horror, unable to make a sound, struggled silently, but he was strong, and there was little she could do. She tried to kick him, but with her bare feet it was of no effect, and she could feel his breath hot against her.

And then, suddenly, someone else was there. The dark man's hold on her loosened, he gave a gasp, and fell backwards, to lie unconscious on the riverbank.

Paul Venter looked at his own fist with satisfaction, for a moment, before he turned to her.

'I regret deeply, ma'am,' he said, formally, 'that a member of this trek should—'

And then he stopped.

'So—' he said, and the warmth had gone from his voice. 'It is you, is it? I might have guessed that where there is trouble, the English girl is likely to be the cause of it.'

Relief from fear had brought Laura close to tears. But she was not prepared to take that.

'That's not fair,' she said unsteadily. 'I just wanted to wash, I didn't know he was there, I didn't know anyone was there.'

Paul Venter's blue eyes looked at her, long, from head to foot.

'I can see that,' he agreed.

Laura felt her cheeks grow warm, as she realised that not only was she standing here in front of this man she disliked so much, in only her petticoat and her bodice, but that somehow, in the struggle, her bodice had been torn.

CHAPTER FOUR

For an eternity, it seemed to Laura, Paul Venter stood there looking at her, with her feet bare, her hair loosened, and her bodice torn. And then, without a word, he lifted her dress from the riverbank, and tossed it to her. She did not thank him, for she did not think she was capable of saying a word.

But it was only when she was safely and decently covered again, that she realised, with dismay, that her problems were not ended. For her dress had buttons down the back. Always, there was either Lisbet or Aletta to do them for her. Now—

She had two choices. One was to go back to the camp with her dress unbuttoned. But the Smit wagon was at the far side, and she would have to walk right across the clearing. The other—

'Mr Venter,' Laura said, as coolly as she could.

'Yes, Miss Conway?' Paul Venter answered, and the mockery in his voice did not make it any easier for her.

'Mr Venter, I shall have to ask you a favour,' she told him.

He waited.

He must know, Laura thought, furiously. He must see—he could make it easier for me.

'Would you mind buttoning my dress for me, please, Mr Venter?' she asked him, and to her shame her voice shook a little. She turned her back to him.

His hands were big, and she could feel that he was having difficulty with the row of small buttons. He did not say that he had finished, but she thought that he must have.

She turned round, knowing that now she would have to thank him.

He was looking down at her, and there was no mockery now in the clear blue eyes.

'You—had better tidy your hair,' he said, his voice strangely tight. 'It is unpinned.'

Laura knew that she must move, that she must do as he said, and pin her hair up again. But she could do nothing. Slowly, Paul Venter put out one hand and lifted a strand of hair back from her face. Then, still slowly, he put both hands on her shoulders and looked down at her.

Afterwards Laura knew, to her shame, that she should have moved away at that moment, she should have said something, done something. But she could do nothing, only stand there, as he came closer to her.

It was only when his lips found hers that she began to struggle to free herself. But his arms held her close to him, and his mouth was warm, and this was no swift stolen kiss such as she had known before, this was a kiss that made the blood sing in her veins, a kiss that made the world narrow to herself and this man. She didn't know when she stopped struggling, when her arms went around his neck to hold him more closely to her. She did not know, either, which of them drew back first, until they were standing there beside the river, looking at each other, and she saw that Paul Venter was as shaken as she was.

'I—must apologise, Miss Conway,' he said, not quite steadily. 'I am afraid I forgot myself, and I forgot—'

He stopped. The hostility was back in his blue eyes, in the tightness of his jaw.

Laura raised her chin.

'And you forgot who I was, Mr Venter,' she returned, and she was inordinately pleased that her voice was steadier than his. But the memory of the way she had returned his kiss could not be dismissed lightly, and she forced herself to go on. 'I—I was also—not quite myself,' she said, with difficulty. 'Can we agree to—to forget the episode?'

'It is already forgotten,' Paul Venter said coolly, formally, and Laura was furious with herself at the strange confusion of feelings that swept through her.

She turned away, and looked down at the unconscious man.

'Will he be all right?' she asked.

The big fair-haired man shrugged.

'His jaw will ache, but he will perhaps have learned a lesson,' he said, unconcernedly. 'But I would advise you, Miss Conway, not to wander away from the camp alone after this.'

Laura, pinning her hair back in place, was relieved not to have to look at him.

'I shall certainly follow your advice,' she told him, and she slipped her feet back into her shoes. 'Are you—are you just going to leave him here?'

Paul Venter bent down and slung the other man over his shoulder.

'I'll take him back to his friends,' he said briefly. And then, sensing her unspoken question—'He will not be likely to say a word of this. Now—I suggest that I go back one way, and you another.'

Without another word, he strode off, the weight of the unconscious man no hindrance to him.

Somewhat to Laura's surprise, she had not been missed, and indeed, she had barely been away from the camp for half an hour. It seemed unbelievable to her that so little time had passed. It also seemed unbelievable that Lisbet noticed nothing strange or different about her. The only comment she made, was on Laura's colour.

'Laura, dear,' she said, softly, 'you have been forgetting your sunbonnet again, your face is quite pink. I guarantee that you will have more freckles by tomorrow. We shall try buttermilk tonight, but I am rather afraid the damage is already done.'

That night, Laura slept less well than she usually did. She was disturbed to find that the memory of being attacked by the dark man was more easily dismissed than the memory of Paul Venter's arms around her, and his lips on hers. And that is ridiculous, she told herself firmly. It was only because I was upset, because I had been frightened, that I—that I responded as I did. It meant nothing more than that. And as for him—I am certain that he is the kind of man who would kiss any girl, given the chance.

It was always at that point that she thought of the moment when she should have drawn back, when she should have stopped him. And although she told herself again that she had not been in her usual frame of mind, that she had been disturbed and confused after being attacked, she had to come to the reluctant conclusion that perhaps Paul Venter had not been entirely to blame.

It is over, I will think no more of it, she told herself, and she turned and buried her face in the big feather pillow, envious of Aletta's blonde sleeping head beside her.

*   *   *

There was plenty of game on the plain, and each day the men rode off to hunt. Paul Venter was always one of the hunters, and Stephen usually joined them. It was sundown when they returned, and by then the wagons were encamped, the oxen unyoked, and the women busy with the evening meal. Laura could not help being relieved that Stephen was usually back late, and that there was little opportunity for them to be alone, for she knew that he would speak to her again.

The night after her encounter at the river, Lisbet came to her as she was climbing into the wagon where Dirkie was already asleep.

'You are retiring early tonight, Laura,' she said. Laura felt her cheeks grow warm, and she was suddenly certain that Lisbet had seen Stephen's purposeful approach around the ring of small fires, and had seen, too, Laura's retreat.

'Laura, dear,' her stepmother went on, and there was laughter in her voice, 'you are not going to tell me that you are tired, a girl who was just complaining so bitterly that she was not allowed to ride off over the plains with the men, and hunt?'

'No, I cannot say I am tired, Lisbet,' Laura admitted. She hesitated, unwilling to hurt Lisbet's feelings, for she knew how fond Lisbet was of her cousin Stephen. And then, because there had always been honesty between herself and this woman who had married her father, she went on with difficulty—'It is Stephen, I—I do not wish to have to give him any answer, because—'

She stopped.

'Because?' Lisbet prompted, gently.

Laura sighed.

'Because I do not know what answer I want to give him,' she said, truthfully.

'He is a good young man, Laura,' her stepmother said, after a moment. 'He is kind, and he is thoughtful. I—I think your father would have liked him.'

In the half-darkness of the wagon, Laura looked down at her slim brown hands, ringless, clasped together.

'I am certain that he would,' she agreed, her voice low. 'But—I just am not certain, Lisbet.'

Her stepmother had always allowed her to use her given name, for there were only fourteen years between the two of them. Now, Lisbet Conway put out one hand and smoothed her stepdaughter's hair back from her face.

'Then you must wait until you are certain, Laura,' she said, and the quiet decision in her voice soothed some of the tumult in Laura's heart. 'A good marriage is worth waiting for. I had a good marriage, and I want you to have one.' And then, with a lightness that reminded Laura how few the years between them were, she went on, 'Perhaps Stephen is too kind and too patient. Perhaps it would suit you better if he were to sweep you off your feet a little?'

Laura smiled.

'I doubt that sweeping me off my feet would be Stephen's way,' she replied, and as she said it, there was the sudden, unbidden thought of another man, a man whose way was very different from Stephen Smit's.

Lisbet stood up.

'In any case, Laura,' she said, with unaccustomed firmness, 'you are not giving yourself or Stephen a chance, if you hide from him. I know you do not want him to declare himself, but surely you are able to talk to him in a friendly way, and make it clear, with tact and with delicacy, how you feel?'

With reluctance, Laura stood up as well.

'There is also Aletta,' she said, as they climbed down the wagon steps.

For a moment, Lisbet was silent.

'Yes, there is Aletta,' she agreed. 'But I wonder, sometimes, if Aletta has become more determined that Stephen should be hers since you came, since he showed so clearly that he prefers you. In any case, tonight she is talking merrily to the younger Marais son. Come, Laura, sit by the fire—you do not have to talk to Stephen unless you want to.' Her lips brushed Laura's forehead. 'You must not feel that you are not part of us, dear—you are my daughter, and everyone knows it!'

Impulsively, Laura hugged her stepmother, once again warmed and impressed by the core of firmness and understanding in this small, gentle woman her father had loved.

'What would I do without you, Lisbet?' she said, not quite steadily.

And Lisbet was right, she found. Stephen did seem content just to sit with her, to talk to her of the trek, of what they might find at Graaff-Reinet when they reached there, of the little group of children she taught each day. When it was time to go to bed, he took her to the wagon and stood at the steps with her. Lisbet and Tante Martha were already inside, Laura could hear them moving quietly, preparing for the night. But Aletta would come, and although there was still no friendship between the two of them, at least there was no further enmity, and Laura certainly did not wish Aletta to find her here saying goodnight to Stephen in the darkness. So she bid him goodnight quickly, in spite of the disappointment in his voice, and by the time Aletta came, she was already curled into the huge feather mattress, pretending to be asleep.

The next morning, however, Laura found that she had, in fact, underestimated Stephen. He was waiting for her before they started, and as they drank coffee together, she realised that there was an unexpected firmness in his voice, decision in his grey eyes.

'Laura,' he said to her, 'in a few days we shall be at Graaff-Reinet, and there will be many other trekkers there.' He paused, and there was now a momentary uncertainty in his voice, and this brought an ache to Laura's heart. 'There will be predikants there, Laura —there would even be a minister of your own church. We could be married.'

'Oh Stephen,' Laura began, not quite steadily, 'I don't know what to say. I wish you hadn't asked me—at least not yet—'

She stopped, confused.

'Not yet?' Stephen repeated. 'Then—you are not saying no, Laura?'

'I'm not saying yes,' Laura told him quickly.

He took both her hands in his, and now he was smiling.

'That does not matter,' he said to her. 'As long as you are not saying no, I can wait.'

'Stephen, you must not think—' Laura began, but he shook his head.

'I will not think,' he replied. 'But—I will hope, Laura.'

Long after the party of hunters had ridden off, long after the wagons had begun their steady roll across the plains, Laura was troubled. Had she said more to him than she wanted to—or had he taken too much out of what she had said?

They made that a short day, for they hoped to reach the big camp the following day. Thus Laura sat with her

small band of scholars in the late afternoon, passing the
reading-book round the group, asking spellings, writing
numbers in the dust. And once again, as before, she was
conscious that she was being watched. Not by the dark
man, she knew—he and his friends had ridden off, to
join with another trek. She forced herself not to look up.

A shadow fell over the small group.

'Good afternoon, Miss Conway,' Paul Venter said.

Laura said nothing, furious at her own confusion,
furious that she could do no more than give a small
inclination of her head.

'It is my turn to ask a favour of you,' he said, and
colour flew into her cheeks at this reminder that she had
had to ask him to button her dress for her. And the
reminder of what had followed that.

'My little sister would very much like to join your
scholars,' he said, and she saw that it was not easy for
him to ask. 'She has seen the other children coming, and
she longs to join them. She—is lonely.'

'Then of course she may,' Laura told him, her hostility
forgotten at the thought of a child being lonely. 'Do
bring her—we'd love to have her, wouldn't we,
children?'

Paul Venter smiled down at the children as they
assented, and Laura thought, in spite of herself, that his
smile made him seem so much younger. Not, of course,
that the smile was directed at her, she reminded herself
hastily.

'She has been ill,' he told Laura quietly, 'and she is still
far from strong. She—cannot do much more than lie in
the wagon. Our parents are dead, we travel with an aunt
and uncle.'

In spite of herself, Laura turned to watch his tall figure
stride across the clearing, the thick fair hair bright in the

sunshine. When he came back, though, he walked slowly, and carried the child in his arms with care. Although he had said she had been ill, Laura was unprepared for the frailty of the little girl, the blue eyes seeming too large for her pale face.

'There, Mariette,' Paul Venter said, setting her down gently. And there was an unexpected ache in Laura's throat at the sight of his big brown hands on the child's golden hair. 'When Miss Conway has finished, I shall come and carry you back.'

At first, little Mariette sat silent, looking from one child to another. But by the end of the lesson she was replying, if a little shyly, and she even laughed with the other children, when Laura pretended to do a sum wrong and had to be corrected.

'Thank you, Miss Conway,' Paul Venter said, with some difficulty, as he stood ready to go, the child in his arms.

'I loved having her,' Laura said, meaning it. 'See you tomorrow, Mariette.'

The next day, though, there was to be little thought of school. For as they neared the big camp at the village of Graaff-Reinet, the hunting party, who had ridden ahead, could be seen riding back towards the wagons, hard and furious, in a cloud of dust. Oom Jan's wagon was the first, and the leading rider reined in beside him. It was Paul Venter.

'Trouble, Oom Jan,' he said, grimly. 'I have just spoken to the Nels' trek, ahead of us. They were stopped by soldiers, searched, and all their gunpowder was taken. They were allowed to proceed, but without powder.'

Laura, who had been sitting beside the old man, saw his hands tighten on the reins.

'But how can they expect us to go among the Kaffirs and the Zulus with no gunpowder to defend ourselves?' he asked. 'And none to use for hunting game for food?'

'That does not worry the English,' Paul Venter said, and for one brief moment, his eyes rested on Laura. 'Whether we live or die as we trek is nothing to them. Now, what are we to do? They know we carry gunpowder, there is no point in trying to hide it and then come back for it. They will search the wagons until they find it.'

'Then you must let them find it,' Laura said, leaning forward.

The other horsemen had reined in as well, and there was suspicion on every face.

'Not all of it,' Laura said, impatiently. 'I mean let them find a little, but we must hide the bulk of it. Let them find enough to satisfy themselves, but we will still have the rest.'

Of all the men, it was only Paul Venter who realised immediately what she meant.

'Yes,' he said, slowly. 'Yes, that would be the way. But where are we to hide the gunpowder?'

Laura's mind whirled. Where indeed? It had to be a safe place, and yet it had to be done swiftly.

'Under the mattresses, here in the wagon,' she said. 'There where Tante Martha sits.'

The old woman, her sweet, placid face bewildered, looked up from the feather mattress. Paul Venter looked at her.

'It might do,' he said, doubtfully. And then he turned and looked down at Laura. 'When the English soldiers come,' he said to her, 'where will your loyalties be?'

Tears stung Laura's eyes.

'Do you dare to think that I would give you away?' she

said to him, and without waiting for an answer, she turned away.

For the next half hour, there was feverish activity, as the gunpowder was brought to the Smits' wagon and hidden under the large feather mattresses. To make room for it, some of the clothes packed there had to be taken to other wagons. Also enough gunpowder had to be left to allay suspicions.

It was barely done, and Tante Martha back in her place, when Stephen came riding up to tell them the soldiers were coming. Immediately, on a word of command, the wagons began to move, and by the time the small band of soldiers reached them, they had covered another mile.

Laura, sitting inside the wagon with Tante Martha, Lisbet and Aletta, heard Paul Venter reply to the English captain. It was the first time, she realised, she had heard him speak English. He spoke it well, so it was obviously choice, and not lack of ability and fluency, that made him prefer his own tongue.

'And how are we to proceed, in frontier country, with no gunpowder, Captain?' he asked coolly.

'I have my orders,' was the reply. 'There is trouble enough ahead, without all you people going up there and stirring up more.'

'We have no intention of stirring up trouble—but we should be able to defend ourselves,' Paul Venter replied. 'And how are we to hunt for game, without gunpowder? We need meat, you know that.'

There was silence, and Laura could imagine the big fair-haired Boer staring at the band of English soldiers.

'My orders are to search,' the Englishman said. 'We shall start at the back.'

Laura longed to peep out, to try to see what was

happening, for it seemed an endless time that there was nothing but muffled sounds. Occasionally there was a shout of triumph, and she knew that would be when the soldiers found some of the gunpowder that had been deliberately hidden, but not too well-hidden. And then they were working on the wagon behind, searching carefully. And Laura's heart sank in dismay, for they had made the women get out, and they were lifting the mattresses. If they did the same in this wagon—

Risking being seen, she opened the canvas and peeped out, for there was a thought in her mind, a familiarity in the English Captain's voice. There he was, standing watching as his men searched. If he would only turn—Yes. She was right, it was Captain Seton.

She moved back to sit beside Lisbet, wondering what best to do. And then she heard the soldiers outside their own wagon.

'But you have searched the baggage stowed underneath,' Oom Jan was protesting. 'And my wife is inside —she has been unwell. Surely you need not disturb her?'

'I have my orders,' the Captain said again, brusquely, but not unsympathetically. 'I regret, sir, but the women must dismount.'

'Wait,' Laura whispered to the others. And then, without giving herself time to think, she moved to the front of the wagon, opened the flap, and climbed out. The soldiers turned at the movement.

Laura, forcing herself to remain calm and composed, sat on the bench, and held out her hand to the Captain.

'Good afternoon, Captain Seton,' she said, sweetly. 'Do you remember me? Laura Conway.' And then, deliberately, she added—'Captain Conway's daughter.'

There was recognition and utter surprise on his face. And behind him, on Paul Venter's face, Laura saw suspicion and distrust, as he wondered, all too obviously, if he had been wrong to trust her, the daughter of an English Captain.

CHAPTER
FIVE

'MISS Conway!' Captain Seton said, his astonishment obvious. 'What in all the world are you doing here?'

Laura began to dismount from the wagon, and the English Captain moved forward to help her.

'Thank you, Captain Seton,' Laura said, and to her relief her voice was steady. She looked around at the group of trekkers, and she hoped that the strain and the tension so evident to her, was less evident to the English Captain. For a moment, her eyes met Paul Venter's, then she turned back to the Captain. 'Can we talk alone, Captain Seton?' she said, her voice low.

'Of course, Miss Conway,' he said, unable to hide his bewilderment. 'No—the search can wait, men.'

There was some small shade afforded by the wagon, and Laura led the way there.

'You find my presence here surprising, Captain Seton,' she said, and she tried to smile.

'I could not believe my eyes,' the Captain admitted. 'You—Captain Conway's daughter—here in this group of Boer trekkers!' He hesitated, and then, somewhat awkwardly, went on—'Of course, I heard about your father. He was a brave man, Miss Conway, and a fine soldier. I am afraid I gave the matter no thought, but I would have presumed you to have returned to England.'

Laura put her hand on his arm.

'Thank you for saying that about my father,' she said, and now it needed much more of an effort to keep her voice steady. 'You have perhaps forgotten that my stepmother is the daughter of a frontier Boer? When —when my father died, I came to live with her people, and—since they trek, I trek with them.'

The Captain hesitated for only a moment.

'Miss Conway,' he said, earnestly, 'you have not had the pleasure of meeting my wife, for I married after leaving Cape Town, but I assure you that you would find a welcome in our home.' There was genuine concern in his grey eyes, 'It is unthinkable that Captain Conway's daughter should be left here in the company of people who do not even speak English unless they are forced to!'

His unexpected kindness touched Laura more than she would have thought possible.

'I thank you most sincerely, Captain Seton,' she said, with difficulty. 'But these people have been kind to me, and—I could not leave my stepmother and my small brother. No, it is entirely by choice that I go with them. But—but the old lady in the wagon—surely you will not distress her by asking her to dismount?'

'I would not dream of it,' the Captain assured her. 'Your being here changes things entirely, Miss Conway.'

For a moment, his eyes clouded.

'You must understand, I have my orders. I know that it is hard to expect people to travel further with little or no ammunition for protection, but that is my command.' He took her hand, and bowed over it. 'Your party may now proceed, Miss Conway, without any further search. We have found, in any case, sufficient ammunition to prove that we searched, although it may surprise my superiors that a party this size should travel with so little.

I shall, of course, explain as well that Captain Conway's daughter is one of the members of this party.'

In that moment, Laura was certain that the Captain was in no way deceived. And further, that he was carrying out orders that he had no heart for in removing the means of defence from the parties of Boers.

'I—thank you, Captain Seton,' she said quietly.

'I—trust you have made the right decision, Miss Conway,' he said in return. 'I made that offer in all sincerity.'

For a moment, Laura thought of how it would be. She would fit in easily to the garrison life, for she had never known anything else until she came to the frontier. There would be tea-parties, and there would be dances, and there would be young officers vying for the pleasure of her company. In time, no doubt, there could well be marriage to one of those young officers.

And what had she chosen, instead of that?

The danger and the uncertainty of the trek, the necessity at some time of giving an answer to Stephen, the hostility of Aletta, and the resentment of many of the other members of the party because she was English. But—there was Lisbet, and there was Dirkie. There was Tante Martha, and that moment of understanding and closeness in the tiny graveyard of Morgenster. There was the memory of that moment on the pass, when the mists cleared, and the air was crisp around them.

'Thank you, Captain Seton,' she said, steadily. 'But I am confident that I have made the right decision.'

Once again he bowed, and then he turned round, gave a sharp command to his soldiers, and a few moments later they were riding away. Laura closed her eyes, and a wave of relief swept over her. She could hear the others in the party talking, and one or two of the men came to her and thanked her, more than a little awkwardly. The preparations were made for the trek to get under way again.

But Paul Venter stood beside Laura, looking down at her. His clear blue eyes were cool, and his voice suspicious.

'You were an uncommonly long time speaking to the English Captain, Miss Conway,' he said abruptly. 'I should have thought your—powers of persuasion to be more effective than that.'

Laura felt her throat grow tight at the cool dislike in his voice. Not that I care, she told herself hastily, what a man as arrogant as this thinks of me.

She lifted her head, and she knew that her cheeks were warm with resentment.

'If you must know, Mr Venter,' she told him, her voice as cool as his own, 'Captain Seton was—commiserating with me on the loss of my father, and he was also offering me a home with himself and his wife.'

'Which you refused?' Paul Venter asked, unbelieving.

'Which I refused,' Laura agreed.

The big fair man said nothing, but his very silence was enough. Suddenly Laura was angry.

'I should not complain, if I were you, Mr Venter,' she said. 'Whatever means I used, I did succeed in saving your precious ammunition.'

She turned, then, and would have walked away, so that he should not see the tears of anger in her eyes. But his hand on her arm held her fast, and unwillingly she was swung round towards him.

'Just remember, Miss Conway,' he said evenly, 'that my "precious ammunition" as you call it, will serve to save the lives of most of the men, women and children on this trek. Including you.'

And now he was the one to turn away. As she

watched, he swung himself into the saddle of his horse and rode off, his wide-brimmed hat pushed back on his sunbleached hair.

The remainder of the journey to Graaff-Reinet was uneventful, and towards sunset they were able to outspan in the large clearing where there were other parties already encamped. That night was different from the previous nights on trek, for now the parties gathered together in the wide circle of the wagons, and there were fires, and music, and dancing. Laura refused to dance that night, partly because she was indeed tired, but also because dancing would mean dancing with Stephen, and she wanted to avoid that, as she wanted to avoid any further problems with Aletta. And so she sat beside Lisbet and Tante Martha, watching Aletta, her golden curls swinging, her fair skin flushed with pleasure as she moved gracefully from partner to partner. Dirkie, allowed to stay up later than usual, was soon drowsy, and Laura held him close to her, until at last he fell asleep. Laura looked down at him, her heart aching with love for this small brother who grew more and more like their father with each passing day. Gently, she smoothed the hair back from his forehead. As she did so, she was all at once conscious of being watched. She lifted her head. Paul Venter sat across the circle from her, and in the glow of the leaping flames, there was, for a moment, no hostility, no resentment, on his face.

It seemed to Laura that her heart had stopped beating, for everything was so still. Almost, she thought, as if for that endless moment, the whole world had stopped.

And then the flame burned brighter, and Paul Venter turned away, and she told herself, with severity, that she must not have such foolish fancies.

'I think I will put Dirkie to bed,' she told her step-mother, 'and I will stay in the wagon as well. It is late and I am tired.'

Lisbet did not try to persuade her to stay, and Laura hardened her heart against the disappointment in Stephen's face when he saw her rise. At the steps of their own wagon she turned, with the sleeping child in her arms.

The firelight gleamed on the faces of the dancers, and of those sitting watching. Aletta was still dancing, and she was having such a good time that she would be sure to be in a pleasant mood, Laura thought with relief, for Aletta in a bad mood was something to be avoided. Paul Venter was dancing now as well, she could see his fair head at the far side, and she could see that he was smiling down at the small dark girl he was dancing with. Tante Martha, she could see, was drowsy, and no doubt would soon come to bed as well. Lisbet was talking to Piet Marais, from a farm which had been near Morgenster. He was, Laura thought, a few years older than Lisbet, a widower and a quiet man. For a moment, as she watched Lisbet talking to him, a disquieting thought struck Laura. But no, she told herself firmly, that was a foolish thing to think, for how could Lisbet even think of any other man, when she had been married to John Con-way? No, she was being neighbourly, there was nothing more than that to it.

The next day, there was a chance to see the little settlement of Graaff-Reinet. Laura liked it, with its air of order and neatness, with its clean, white-washed houses set out neatly in rows, and its wide avenues of orange and lemon trees. And she liked the bustle around the encampment, as all the pedlars came with their wares and the women crowded round, eager to see, and eager to buy, for this would be their last chance of such buying.

Among the men, there was time for buying only necessities, for this was the time for talking, for making decisions on the question of whether or not each trek was to continue as it was, or was to join with a larger party.

They remained in Graaff-Reinet for another day and night, and at the end of that time, the men of the party decided that they would travel on as they had been, rather than joining a larger party.

'We could join Retief's trek,' Stephen told Laura, 'for that is what we intended doing. But although we intend travelling in much the same direction, and although we will not be much distant from them, we have decided to go on as we are.' He hesitated, and then, his eyes on her face, went on—'When we left, our idea of joining with Retief was because he is a leader, and—a trek needs a leader, a strong man who will put down trouble at the first sign. Oom Jan is not that man, for much as I admire and respect him, I know that he is not quick enough to take a decision, and perhaps not hard enough. And—I am not that man. But we have a leader in Paul Venter.'

Laura was furious with herself at her inability to control the wave of warm colour she could feel in her cheeks.

'I do not see why you could not be as good a leader as Paul Venter, Stephen,' she said. 'you are every bit as good a man as he, and much better.'

Stephen smiled.

'Thank you for your loyalty, Laura,' he said. 'But we must be honest and clear-sighted where the welfare of the trek is concerned. No, we have our leader in Paul Venter, and I for one am prepared to follow his orders.'

'Well, I certainly have no intention of being ordered around by him!' Laura replied, lifting her chin high. 'He may be a good leader, but I find a great deal left to be desired in his behaviour in other ways!'

The whole party rose early the following morning, before sunrise, ready to move off from the little settlement. The other men of the party seemed to have no trouble accepting Paul Venter as their leader, and Laura, standing beside the fire drinking coffee and eating a rusk, watched as he stood, too far from her to hear what was said, but obviously telling this man what to do, and that man where his duties lay. Then, as he spoke, he looked across and saw her, and with a brief word to his companions, left them and strode across the clearing to her.

'Good morning, Miss Conway,' he said, formally. 'I wish to take this opportunity of asking you if you will please continue with your lessons for the children. I—we are all very grateful to you for doing this.'

It had not been easy for him to say this, Laura could see. But perversely, she was not prepared to accept it.

'Thank you, Mr Venter,' she replied coolly, 'but I teach the children because I wish to. I need neither your permission nor your approval for that.'

For a moment, she saw reluctant admiration, tinged with something that she feared was amusement, in his clear blue eyes.

He bowed.

'I accept that you feel that way, Miss Conway,' he said. 'But let us get one thing clear right now.' And there was now nothing but cool hostility as he looked down at her. 'I have been chosen to lead this trek, and I will do it to the best of my ability. But I insist on obedience and acceptance of my leadership—from you as well as from everyone else, Miss Conway. You will remember that.'

And then, with no apparent haste, he left her and rejoined the men at the far side of the fire. Laura, furious and resentful, and yet at the same time admitting with reluctance that he had been fairly restrained in the way he had made his point, finished her coffee as if the matter was of no concern to her. But when she went back to the wagon, she could not help noticing that her hands were not quite steady.

'I dislike that man thoroughly,' she said to Lisbet, as Paul Venter rode past, doffing his hat to them. 'He is uncivilised and—and arrogant.'

'Those are strong words, Laura,' her stepmother replied, mildly. 'I am sure there is a great deal of good in Paul Venter. Look at the way he is with little Mariette. I have seen few grown men as tender with a child, and that child a sister, as he is.'

Laura had no reply to that, for it was true. Each day, when Paul Venter brought the frail child to Laura for her lessons, his big brown hands were gentle as he set Mariette down and as he lifted her up when they had finished. And there was no doubt that Mariette adored her brother. Her blue eyes—a different blue from his, a softer blue—would light up when he appeared, and she would tell him eagerly all that she had learnt that day. Paul would listen, his hat pushed back on his fair hair, his blue eyes intent in the brown of his face. And then, carefully, he would carry Mariette back to the wagon she shared with their aunt.

They were three days out of Graaff-Reinet when it became all to obvious that the sky was darkening with storm clouds. Anxiously they all scanned the troubled sky, and tried to hurry the oxen on, so that they might reach a more sheltered place to camp for the night.

Laura, weary of sitting in the wagon, was walking beside it when Paul Venter reined in his horse beside her.

'I think you should go into the wagon, Miss Conway,' he told her, almost shouting above the roar of the wind. 'We are in for a bad storm, and it will strike very soon.'

Laura, who had been until then of a mind to give up walking and join the other women in the wagon, felt on hearing Paul Venter say this that she would rather walk.

She opened her mouth to say so, and the big fair man, presumably seeing the signs of mutiny on her face, leaned down, lifted her up, and without a word deposited her in the back of the wagon. Laura, furious, could not even give herself the satisfaction of a reply, for immediately he wheeled his horse around and rode off, checking on the other wagons. The amusement on Aletta's face did little to help matters. But suddenly, there was no time to think of anything else, for as Laura began to help Lisbet to fasten the canvas at the back of the wagon, they saw, far over the plain, a whirling column of dust, coming nearer to them with every second. There was a strange whistling in the wind, and suddenly, with unbelievable force, Laura was flung against her stepmother, and the whole wagon seemed to rock. Then it regained its balance, and in the same instant, they heard somewhere ahead of them the sharp rending of wood.

Almost afraid to look, Laura opened the canvas. For a moment, in the confusion, she thought that nothing had happened, and then she saw that the wagon two ahead of them lay on its side, the shafts broken and the oxen terrified, struggling to free themselves. Then Paul Venter was there, giving orders, calming the oxen, and organising a team of men to set the wagon right again.

With reluctant admiration, Laura had to admit that this was a man who had the ability to get things done, to create order from chaos. An hour later, they had reached a small koppie which provided them with some shelter from the still-strong wind, and the usual nightly preparations were being made. The occupants of the wagon—Simon Botha and his wife Marie, and their three children, had been very fortunate and had escaped with little more than bruises, but the wagon would have to be repaired, and that would take most of the following day, Paul told the silent and sobered group of trekkers around the fires that night. The day could be usefully employed, he said, by a shooting party collecting as much meat as possible, for there was no telling how well stocked with game the region ahead was.

Stephen Smit was one of the shooting party, and Laura, ashamed of her thoughts, could not help but be relieved that he would not be at the camp during the day. For she was certain that he was now determined to talk to her again, and she knew that the moment could not be avoided forever. Sometimes it seemed to her that it would perhaps be the best thing if she were to accept the proposal that Stephen longed to make, if she were to marry him. Many times she told herself that she should regard herself as fortunate to have the attention and affection of a man like Stephen. But as often as she thought this, there would be the memory of that moment of realisation, of longing for an unknown man who would make the blood sing in her veins when he took her in her arms.

And always, with that memory, there was another, a memory she would suppress as swiftly as she could. For it was foolish to think, in the same moment, of the unknown man she would some day find and love and of a man like Paul Venter. That day—the day he had kissed her—she had been upset, distraught, she reminded herself firmly. Not herself. In a susceptible frame of mind. That was all.

The day after the wagon damaged by the whirlwind was repaired, they came to a river in a valley. There was a crossing, fairly shallow, the scouts reported, and a willow-wood pont to take the wagons and the sheep across. The cattle, unwilling and fearful, swam across and huddled together on the far side. The sheep, just as fearful, made a great noise as they were ferried over. Most of the men rode over, their horses swimming from halfway, where the water grew deeper. The women crossed in the wagons, poled over on the pont.

As the wagons reached the far side where there was a steep slope, two teams of oxen were ready to pull them up. Before this, the women were assisted out to take a winding path up the bank, rather than sit in the wagon while it was hauled up by the oxen.

When it came to Laura's turn to be helped ashore, she was dismayed to find Paul Venter standing there, up to his thighs in water. He had just lifted Dirkie and then Lisbet from the wagon, and now they were being helped up the path. Laura, still on the pont, looked at Paul Venter.

'I would rather be assisted by someone else,' she said, coolly. 'I shall wait.'

Paul Venter's jaw was hard.

'That you will not,' he told her brusquely. 'You will take the same treatment as everyone else. Come here.'

Before Laura could resist, he had taken her in his arms, and was carrying her across to the bank. And Laura, once more held close to this man, found that she was again suffering from the same problem in breathing.

'Mr Venter,' she said, with some difficulty, 'there is no need to hold me so tightly, I can barely breathe.'

Paul Venter stopped.

'I beg your pardon, Miss Conway,' he said, 'if I am holding you too tightly. I shall soon remedy that.'

For a moment, she saw the expression in his blue eyes, but she did not guess.

Then, deliberately, he loosened his hold on her, and she fell into the water.

It wasn't deep, but she lost her balance, so that the river water covered her for a moment and she gasped, thus swallowing more water. Then two strong hands were around her wet and muddy waist, and Paul Venter lifted her to her feet.

'I do beg your pardon, Miss Conway,' he said smoothly. 'A most regrettable accident.'

But the laughter in his blue eyes told her, as she already knew, that it was certainly no accident.

CHAPTER
SIX

'PAUL Venter, that was no accident!' Laura said, furiously. 'You meant to let me fall in the water.'

'An accident, I assure you, Miss Conway,' Paul Venter repeated. With exaggerated care, he carried her the short distance to the bank and set her down. Then he turned to Lisbet. 'My apologies, Mrs Conway, for allowing your stepdaughter to fall in the water. I do urge you to see that she changes her wet and—' He looked down at Laura, consideringly. 'Yes, rather muddy clothing, before she catches a chill, although fortunately it is fairly warm.'

With a bow worthy of a drawing-room, he stepped back into the water and waded back towards the pont.

'Come, Laura,' Lisbet said, soothingly, 'see, they are now pulling the wagon up the river bank, we can change your clothes right away, and you will come to no harm.'

'No physical harm, perhaps,' Laura agreed, following her stepmother up the bank, 'but oh, Lisbet, can you not imagine the shame of being dropped into the river, and it so muddy, in front of everyone? Did I not tell you what an insufferable and unbearable man Paul Venter is?'

'He did say it was an accident,' Lisbet murmured.

Laura sniffed.

'It was no accident,' she assured the older woman. 'I can tell you it gave Paul Venter great pleasure to see me spluttering and struggling in the water.'

'You did look funny, Laura,' Dirkie, at her side, agreed with enthusiasm. 'Like swimming with your clothes on. Mother, Mr Venter said it is fairly warm, could I not also swim? I needn't keep my clothes on, though, I could just swim. May I, Mother?'

They had reached the wagon, now freed from the team of oxen which had hauled it up from the river bank and now gone back for the next wagon. Lisbet looked down at her small son.

'No, Dirkie,' she told him, firmly, 'you may not swim. One member of this family swimming today is quite enough, thank you!'

Laura looked at her stepmother.

'It wasn't funny, Lisbet,' she said, for it seemed to her that there was a suspicious twitch at Lisbet's lips.

'Oh no, not at all, dear,' her stepmother agreed hastily.

But Aletta made no attempt to hide her amusement.

'If you had seen yourself, Laura,' she said when Laura came out of the wagon, clean and changed. 'It was extremely funny. I was positively aching with laughter.'

Laura swept past her.

'Then I hope you have recovered without doing yourself an injury,' she returned coldly. Her anger at Paul Venter returned in even greater force. To think that he had made her the butt of Aletta's amusement, and of others. And most of all, of his own, for she could not forget the laughter in his blue eyes as he stood there looking down at her.

Stephen was far from amused. He had not seen the incident but he had heard of it. But, somewhat to Laura's surprise, he was not entirely disposed to believe that it had been no accident.

'I can see no reason why Paul Venter should wish

to—drop you in the river, Laura,' he said, surprised. 'Surely he lost his footing—I know these river pebbles are slippery. I can only wish that I had been there, to have lifted you in safety myself. I assure you, Laura, I would not have slipped, with such a precious burden.'

Warm colour rose in Laura's cheeks, more at the depth of sincerity in Stephen's voice, than at the words.

'I am sorry, too that you were not there, Stephen,' she said, her voice low. She refused to allow herself to remember that moment before Paul Venter let her fall in the river, that moment when his arms held her tightly, close to him, and she had felt his heart beating.

Stephen was still looking down at her, and there was a question in his eyes, a question that Laura did not even want to understand.

'How is your mother, Stephen?' she asked quickly, for Stephen's mother had not been well before the trek began, and for most of the time she had kept to her wagon, attended by her sister.

Stephen's dark eyes clouded.

'She is far from well, Laura,' he told her. 'Each day, she seems to lose strength, and I am certain, although she will not admit it, that she has pain. But what could we do? We had to trek, and—and I am very much afraid she would be no better even if we had never left the farm, than she is now.'

'Oh, Stephen, I am sorry,' Laura said unsteadily, ashamed of herself for not having ascertained just how bad his mother was. 'I had no idea she was so ill.' She hesitated, but only for a moment. 'Could I—would it be all right if I went to see her?'

Stephen's face lit up.

'I would be so grateful, Laura,' he replied. 'She sees

hardly anyone, and she is lonely. Tante Martha comes, of course, but she would like to see you.'

Laura had, of course, known Mrs Smit since coming to live at Morgenster, and she, in company with Lisbet and Tante Martha, had been a fairly regular visitor to the Smits' farm. Thus she was shaken by the change in the small, greyhaired woman who lay in the wagon.

'Stephen should have let us know,' she said, kneeling down and taking the sick woman's hands in hers.

Mrs Smit smiled.

'There is little anyone can do, my dear,' she said. 'My sister looks after me well, but of course she has her own family to see to.'

'I could help,' Laura said impulsively. 'The only thing I do is teach the children. When our school time is over, I can come here and help.'

In the days that followed she went as often as she could, and sometimes even travelled in the Smits' wagon. She had never before had the need to do any nursing, but she found an unexpected talent for it, and many times Stephen's mother, lying back against her pillows, would say gratefully that no one else could make her as comfortable as Laura did.

Sometimes, as she went about the business of caring for Mrs Smit, Laura would find the older woman's dark eyes—Stephen's eyes—resting on her. And she was not surprised when one day Mrs Smit spoke to her of Stephen.

'He is a good son, Laura,' she said, softly. 'Since my husband died, Stephen has worked hard, and yet he has never forgotten to be kind and thoughtful.'

'I know that,' Laura agreed, her voice low.

'He—cares for you a great deal, child,' Mrs Smit went on.

Laura was silent.

'It would ease my concern for him, if you and he—' Stephen's mother paused then, looking at Laura.

And Laura, who had become fond of her patient, looked down at her brown and ringless hands.

'Perhaps it might be better,' she said quietly, 'since I am unable to make up my mind, if I were to—to tell Stephen that my answer is no, that he would do better to forget me, and to look for some other girl. This way is not fair to him. I—I am ashamed of myself, Mrs Smit, that because I cannot say yes, I have not had the strength of mind to say no.'

Stephen's mother sat up with difficulty.

'Please, Laura, do not yet do anything as final as that. There is no need for you to send Stephen away from you—he is not overly unhappy with things as they are—and perhaps in time, Laura, you will find that you have grown to love him.'

Because of the pleading in the sick woman's shadowed eyes, Laura agreed. But she made herself a private promise, that she must make her decision before long, and also, that if she saw that Stephen became less content with the uncertainty, she would tell him, once and for all, that she would not marry him. And then, Laura told herself, he would be free to find someone else.

It would not, she knew, be Aletta. Sometimes she thought that if she had been certain that Stephen would turn to Aletta—and yet, at the same time, she knew that she was too fond of Stephen to wish for him a life dependent on Aletta's whims and caprices.

Day after day, the trek moved on, slowly, steadily. Sometimes there were outriders from another trek, and news would be exchanged. And gradually the news became disquieting, for they heard that there were warlike Kaffirs close by. Their own scouts found a solitary wagon, with two dead men beside it, not far from the path they were following.

Each night, now, when they made camp, the wagons were drawn up into a laager, thus affording them as much protection as possible. As many of the sheep and the cattle as would fit, were inside the laager, and those that were not, were protected by barriers of thornbushes.

Paul Venter had the men of the trek drilled in what they were to do in the event of an attack. The women, too, would be needed for re-loading. Night after night, as Laura was dropping off to sleep, she found herself wondering if this was to be the night that the Kaffirs would attack.

When it happened, no one was surprised. On the instant, the whole camp swung into the planned action. The howls of the attacking Kaffirs, and the fearsome noise made by the terrified cattle and sheep, made the blood run cold. But in a way, Laura thought, kneeling behind Oom Jan, ready to re-load his gun for him, it was almost a relief that it had actually happened.

There was no time to look around, no time to do anything but be there, at the ready. Somehow, she was the one who had to re-load for Oom Jan. Tante Martha was too old, Lisbet was looking after Dirkie, and Aletta was cowering on her mattress, terrified.

Suddenly, there was the whistle of an assegai, and a grunt from the old man in front of her.

'Laura—' He tried to say more, but no words would come. The cruel assegai was wedged in his chest. Laura, terrified, tried to pull it out, but she lacked the strength.

'I'll do it. You hold him.'

Paul Venter was beside her, his big hands strong and confident. Laura would not let herself look away, and when the assegai was out, she was ready to staunch the flow of blood as she helped Paul to carry Oom Jan back inside the wagon.

'Tend him,' Paul said briefly to Tante Martha, but even as he said it his eyes met Laura's for a moment, and the truth was there between them. 'Can you shoot, Laura?' he asked her, and it was only later that she realised he has used her name.

'I can try,' she told him. 'The gun's heavy, but if I can wedge it—there, now I can manage.'

'Good,' he said, and then he was gone, on to the next wagon, to find out where help was needed, and who had been hurt.

Laura found that she needed every ounce of her strength to keep the heavy musket steady. Ahead, in the glow of the fires, a dark figure appeared, and she fired. She did not know—and she did not want to know, then or later—if she had hit him, but he disappeared.

Behind her, Lisbet was there to re-load. Again, Laura fired, and again. But never at random, for Paul Venter had impressed upon everyone the necessity of conserving their ammunition. She never knew how long she knelt there, ready to fire, her eyes straining to see through the darkness lit only by the dying fires. And then, slowly, the darkness lightened, and the yells of the attacking Kaffirs grew more distant. But still Laura remained where she was, her eyes searching the growing dawn, her fingers numb.

She did not hear Paul Venter come silently from behind, but somehow when there was a hand on her shoulder, she knew it was him.

'Come, Laura,' he said, quietly. 'It is over. They have gone.'

He was unshaven, and weary, but there was a light of triumph in his clear blue eyes.

'We have taught them a lesson,' he said, as he took the gun from her, and helped her to her feet. Stiff, her limbs aching, Laura would have fallen if he had not caught her. 'You did well, girl,' he told her, and absurdly, after all that there had been between them, her heart lifted at his simple praise.

'And—the price?' she asked him, her voice low.

He shook his head.

'Less than we might have expected,' he replied. 'They got some of our cattle, and a few sheep, and—there are heavier losses than that. The Viljoen brothers, both of them, for it was there that the attack began. Danie Erasmus. And there are some wounded.' His arm, still unaccountably round her shoulders, tightened. 'And —Oom Jan.'

The old man had died within an hour of being wounded, Tante Martha told Laura, in her arms.

'The Lord was merciful,' she said simply, 'for he did not suffer, he lost consciousness. And—I was with him.'

They buried Oom Jan and the other three men that morning, in simple graves, marked only by a lonely thorn tree. Tante Martha was distressed that she could find no mourning black to wear, but Lisbet assured her that there was no disrespect in the circumstances. She and Aletta stood one on each side of their mother, supporting her, while Paul Venter read from the bible, and then, a little awkwardly, said a few words about the bravery and the sacrifice of these men.

'We will not forget them,' he finished simply, and

Lisbet led her mother away as the earth began to fall into the graves.

Laura, with her arm around Dirkie, stood still, and she was proud of the way her small brother behaved himself. He had wept, earlier, for his grandfather, but now his eyes were dry.

'You were very good, Dirkie,' she said to him, as they went slowly back to the wagon.

'I did want to cry,' the child told her, and his hand tightened on hers. 'But you know, Laura, the thing that most of all made me want to cry, was that it made me remember when Father died.'

Laura, too, had been unable to keep that other loss, that other graveside, from her mind, but she had not thought that Dirkie, at six, would have remembered something that happened more than a year ago.

'It made me remember too, Dirkie,' she told him, her voice low. They looked at each other, the small brother and his grown-up sister, and Laura thought—how could I even have considered leaving Dirkie, my own flesh and blood?

It was perhaps because Oom Jan's death had made her thoughts turn more than usual to her father, that she found herself noticing, more and more, her step-mother's growing friendship with the widower Piet Marais. He was one of those who came and offered whatever help he could, now that they were without Oom Jan, and he arranged to have his wagon next to theirs, so that he could be near them if he was needed. There was never anything unseemly in Lisbet's conduct, Laura knew, but sometimes, when she was talking to Piet Marais, when she looked up, smiling, at his arrival, there was more than just neighbourliness, Laura felt certain.

The thought disturbed her. She found herself talking with some coolness to her stepmother, and there had never before been coolness between them. Perhaps not coolness, but certainly some reserve, Laura knew. Lisbet herself said nothing, but Stephen, who had also had his wagon brought nearer to theirs, so that he could divide his attention between his mother and them, noticed it, and talked to her about it.

'Laura, is there something wrong between you and Lisbet?' he asked her one night, with unaccustomed frankness. Laura, taken aback, immediately denied this.

'Laura, Laura,' he said, gently, and he covered her hand with his. 'Lisbet is my cousin, and—you must know how dear you are to me. It distresses me to see that you are—less close than you have always been.'

'There is nothing wrong, nothing at all,' Laura told him, knowing that her colour was heightened.

'I suppose,' he said, turning away to light his pipe, 'that you are disturbed in case she should marry Piet Marais? But why, Laura?'

Laura turned away.

'How could she, when—when she loved my father?' she said, unsteadily, in some ways glad that Stephen had forced her to speak, to admit this.

Now he took both her hands in his.

'It is just because she loved your father, because she had a happy marriage, that she can consider marrying again,' he told her. 'And—she must be lonely, Laura.'

'She has Dirkie, and she has me,' Laura murmured.

'She can still be lonely,' Stephen replied. 'Think of that, Laura. And when you think of loneliness—remember that I too am lonely.'

Before she could do anything to stop him, he took her in his arms and kissed her. And Laura, grateful to him for the way he had talked to her, for his understanding and his thoughtfulness, found that she could return his kiss.

When he let her go, he looked down into her eyes for a long time. And then, seeming not to find what he was looking for, he touched her lips with his once again, briefly, warmly, before he turned and left her.

'You are more likely to catch cold here, Miss Conway, than in the river,' Paul Venter's voice said lazily, from the darkness.

Laura gasped, and swung round.

'How long have you been there?' she asked him, angrily.

There was just enough light for her to see him shrug.

'Long enough,' he told her. 'I must admit I could not hear all the sweet exchanges, but—I could certainly see the fond farewells.'

Laura lifted her chin.

'Any gentleman would have—would have coughed, or made his presence evident,' she told him with resentment.

Now there was laughter in his voice.

'Surely I do not have to remind you, Miss Conway, that I am no gentleman?'

'No, indeed,' Laura returned, and she was proud of the cool steadiness of her voice. 'I need no reminding of that! And you were right, Mr Venter, it is cold. Goodnight.'

It was indeed cold, and it became colder in the following days. It was August, and often, cold as the days were, the nights were worse. The trek was held up by late lambing, for the newlyborn lambs could not keep up the slow but steady pace they had proceeded at. Laura could no longer hold her little class outside, even in the afternoon, and they had to seek shelter in a wagon instead.

One afternoon, she noticed that Paul's little sister, Mariette, seemed unwell. She looked even more frail than usual, and Laura thought that her chest seemed to be congested. The next day Paul did not bring her to the class, so when they had finished, and Laura had attended to Stephen's mother, she went to see how the child was.

Mariette was propped up on pillows, and there were shadows of weariness under her blue eyes, but her small face lit up when Laura, having spoken to her aunt, climbed into the wagon. She sat with Mariette for as long as she could, while her aunt went off to prepare some gruel so that the child would take something. Laura fed it to her, sitting beside her and persuading her to take just one spoonful more.

The next day, when she had finished with the children and with Mrs Smit, she went back again, and now she was even more concerned, for Mariette had a fever. Laura sponged her, and did all she could to cool her down, but the little girl was too weary to take more than a spoonful or so of the gruel. When Laura left her she had fallen into an uneasy sleep. Laura, concerned about her, would have liked to stay there that night. If it had been anyone else, she would not have hesitated.

But that night, she had just retired when Lisbet called her.

'Paul Venter is here, Laura,' she said, softly. 'His sister is ill, and she has asked for you.'

Paul Venter held a lantern, and in its light she could see how worried he was.

'Mariette is very bad,' he told her. 'Will you come, Laura?'

Without a word, Laura pulled a blanket over her gown

and followed him. He strode ahead of her, not waiting to
see if she should stumble or not, but driven, Laura knew,
by anxiety for the sick child.

And sick she certainly was. Far more sick than she had
been in the afternoon. Once again, Laura sponged the
hot little body, and tried to get Mariette to sip some
water. Then, with Paul's help, she propped the little girl
even higher, to try to ease her breathing. It must, she
realised later, have been some hours that she was
there before there was any change. And then, slowly,
Mariette began to breathe more easily, and it seemed to
Laura that she had grown a little cooler.

'I think she's sleeping normally now,' she murmured.

'I think she is,' Paul Venter agreed. For the first time
since she had known this man there was no laughter, no
mockery, no resentment, in his blue eyes. There was
weariness, and—there was gratitude.

'I—do not know how to thank you, Laura,' he said,
quietly. 'You must be worn out—go and rest, I shall
watch her.'

He was exhausted too, she could see.

'Your aunt?' she asked.

'She has her own family,' he told her, with no resentment. 'They are in the wagon next to us—she said I was
to call her if I needed her. But Mariette wanted you.'

Laura stood up, still looking doubtfully at the sleeping
child.

'I will sleep for a little,' she said, 'then I will come
back, and you can sleep.'

'I can go without sleep if it is necessary,' he told her.
'Take the lantern, Laura.'

She did not think he had even realised that he had
used her given name again, for there was room for
nothing in his mind but his little sister. He did not even

turn as Laura went out of the wagon.

She went back to the sky blue wagon and lay down, and she thought that she must have slept. But it was still dark when she awoke, and she crept silently out again, telling herself that she could better do without sleep than Paul Venter could, for he carried the responsibility of the trek.

All was silent in the camp, and when she reached the Venters' wagon, one swift, anxious glance told her that Mariette, asleep, was considerably better.

Her second glance showed her Paul Venter, asleep also, his sunbleached head dropped in weariness on his brown arm, close to Mariette on the piled-up pillows.

He must have been worn out, Laura thought.

And as she watched him, a strange and disturbing thing happened. All her dislike and her resentment of this man were gone, and instead there was a bewildering confusion of feeling she could not even put a name to.

Unable to stop herself, Laura went forward, slowly. She reached out one hand and touched Paul Venter's fair head, gently.

And at her touch, he woke.

CHAPTER
SEVEN

In the light of the lantern in Laura's hand, they looked at each other, the big fair Boer, and the slight English girl.

'Mariette?' Paul Venter asked, his voice still blurred with sleep. Laura realised that he did not know that it was her touch on his head that had awakened him. 'Is she—?'

'She's much better,' Laura told him, as steadily as she could. 'Look, she's sleeping normally now. I came back to sit with her, so that you may sleep.'

And even as she said it, a wave of warm colour flooded her face, for she realised that this was impossible, Paul Venter's bed being at the other side of the wagon.

'Yes, you are right, it would not be quite proper, would it?' the big fair man asked, and there was the old amusement and mockery in his voice, now that his small sister was recovering. 'I think you had better return to your wagon, had you not? Now that Mariette is a little better, surely it would suffice if I rested here, close to her?'

'I am certain it would,' Laura agreed hastily. And then, in case there should be any misunderstanding on his part, 'Of course, it was all right for me to be here earlier with you, when she was so ill, I—I mean, no one would think—everyone would realise that it was necessary for both of us to care for her.'

'I think they would,' Paul Venter replied gravely. He

took the lantern from her, and went with her to the canvas flap of the wagon. There, as he handed the lantern back to her, he looked down at her. 'Laura, I cannot thank you enough for what you have done for Mariette. No one could have done more. And—you an English girl.'

It seemed to Laura that the world had narrowed to herself and this man, standing together there in the dimly-lit wagon.

'We English are people like any other people, Paul,' she said, with some difficulty.

Still he looked down at her, saying nothing.

Afterwards, Laura could never be certain whether he moved towards her, or she towards him, or whether they both moved. But suddenly, violently, he took her in his arms and crushed her to him, his lips seeking hers, his arms holding her ever closer. For one moment, Laura thought of the lantern in her hand, and tried to keep it steady, and then she forgot everything but the warm seeking of Paul Venter's lips.

And then, even more suddenly, he let her go. Laura stumbled, almost losing her balance, but he made no attempt to help her.

'Not quite like any other people, in the things you have done to my people,' he said, not quite steadily, and it took Laura some few moments to remember what she had said to him before he kissed her. 'But that does not alter what you have done for my sister, and I thank you again.'

There was nothing but cold formality in his voice and in his face, and Laura, bewildered and shaken, could scarcely believe that this was the same man whose lips had been on hers, bruising them with his hunger. Without a word she turned and left him, and made her way across the clearing to the Smit wagon. Lying on the soft feather mattress beside Aletta, she was awake until dawn, beyond tears, beyond anything but a dull aching that seemed to go through her entire body.

'You are exhausted, Laura, child,' Lisbet said as they drank their coffee beside the fire, and she tried to persuade Laura to eat a rusk or two. 'Were you long with little Mariette? I meant to stay awake, to ask you how she was, but I did not hear you come back.'

'She is considerably better,' Laura told her carefully, and because it was easier, she gave in and took a rusk from her stepmother. 'I think perhaps the dampness we went through near the riverbed was bad for her. Now that we are climbing, the air might be better for her.'

It was another two days before Mariette was well enough to join the other children for lessons again. During that time, Laura went to see her in the wagon, but only when she was certain that Paul would not be there. And when he did bring the child back for her lessons, he did nothing more than greet her with a formal nod as he set Mariette down beside the others.

I care nothing for him, she told herself, more than once. My first feeling of dislike for him and for his arrogance was completely justified.

It was nothing more than surprise, she decided, that made her turn and walk away a night or two later, when she came on Paul Venter talking to Aletta, Aletta's golden head lifted towards him her fair face flushed. And he was smiling, Laura could not help seeing, in that brief moment before she turned. Smiling down into Aletta's raised face, with an open warmth she had never seen towards herself.

No, I care nothing for him, Laura told herself once

more. And even less, that he can listen to Aletta's foolish chatter!

As soon as she had thought this, she was ashamed at her own lack of charity, and she hastened to remind herself that Aletta was indeed a very pretty girl. And, of course, of his own race—not one of the hated English.

Aletta, unfortunately, had seen Laura turn away, and she made much of this.

'It must be hard for you, Laura, to find that there is at least one man here who does not even wish to hear your name mentioned, for he dislikes you so much!' she taunted Laura the next day. 'I swear, I did no more than wonder why you should have turned without so much as greeting us, and Paul was so violent and so outspoken in his dislike of you, that I found it quite embarrassing.'

'Nonsense, Aletta,' Laura returned with asperity, 'you must have enjoyed every moment.'

'Girls, girls, that is no way to talk!' Lisbet broke in, and it was the hurt in her gentle face that made Laura stop, and hold her tongue even when Aletta would have gone on.

Later that night, when Dirkie was newly asleep, and Laura was alone with her stepmother in the wagon, for Tante Martha and Aletta were still out beside the campfires, she apologised, somewhat awkwardly.

'I did not mean to distress you, Lisbet,' she said, with some difficulty, 'by talking to Aletta as I did.'

'It was not entirely your fault, dear,' Lisbet replied, and Laura was glad that her stepmother would admit that it certainly was in part her fault. 'Aletta set out to goad you, and she succeeded.'

'I should not have let her succeed,' Laura said, her voice low. 'It would have been more dignified if I had remained silent.'

'It would indeed,' Lisbet agreed, and she smiled. 'But I doubt that dignity has ever been your strong point, Laura. And although Aletta has now accepted that whether or not you and Stephen marry he will not be in love with her, she still resents you for that. She will always think that you took him away from her, although I am certain he was never hers to take.'

Laura looked down at her clasped hands, brown from the many hours spent in the open air.

'If I thought that she had ever really loved Stephen,' she said, quietly, 'then I would indeed feel very bad. But Lisbet, surely it is no more than her pride that is hurt?'

'I think you are right,' the older woman agreed, after a moment. 'But Laura, never underestimate Aletta's hostility to you. She is my own sister, but I know that she is spoiled, that she must always have her own way, and if she cannot have it, then it is the worse for everyone around her.' She stood up. 'Come, my dear, Dirkie is fast asleep, let us rejoin the others for a little, before we go to bed.'

'Lisbet—wait,' Laura said, putting out a hand to hold her stepmother back. 'I—I have been wanting to talk to you.'

Lisbet sat down again, her eyes on Laura's face.

'I—I do not find this easy to say,' Laura began, with a great deal of awkwardness, 'but—I am sorry I was a little strange, a little distant with you, a few days ago.'

Her stepmother's dark eyes were gentle.

'You were unhappy about my friendship with Piet Marais,' she said, and it was not a question. 'I saw that, Laura, but it was difficult for me to know how to talk to you about it, difficult to know what to say. And then, just when I was determined that I could not let matters go on like that between you and me, you changed, and you were once again my warm and loving Laura.'

Quietly, Laura told her of what Stephen had said to her, of the way he had made her see that she must not close her mind to the thought of Lisbet marrying again. But she had said nothing of what Stephen had said at the end, about loneliness, and she said nothing of his reference to his own loneliness, or of his kiss.

'Stephen made me see that I had been selfish, Lisbet,' she said at last. And then, looking directly into Lisbet's face, she said, quietly—'I do not think my father would want you to spend the rest of your life alone.'

Lisbet's eyes filled with tears.

'Thank you for that, Laura,' she said, unsteadily. She tried to smile. 'Of course, at the moment there is really nothing to discuss, for there is nothing but friendship between a lonely man and a lonely woman.'

So Stephen was right, Lisbet was lonely. Painfully, with new insight, Laura saw well how that could be, that Lisbet should be lonely, in spite of having her small son and her grown stepdaughter, and even her parents. When a woman had known a close and a loving companionship with a man, and when she was then left alone . . .

As I may well be alone, she thought, with sudden and stabbing clarity. But—could it be enough, to agree to marry someone because you are afraid of being alone? Could it be fair, to—to a man like Stephen?

Stephen's mother had said nothing more to Laura of her hopes, but sometimes, when Laura was caring for her and Stephen came, Laura would see the sick woman's eyes go from her son to the girl he had grown to love, with a silent question, an unspoken plea. And Laura, unable to answer the question or the plea, would have to turn away.

Each day, steadily, the trek moved on, and sometimes it seemed to Laura that she had never known any other life than this, the rhythm of the day's march with the wagons. After the early start, the stop and the outspan and encampment in the late afternoon, and her time with the children, trying to teach them their letters and their numbers before they were set free to run and play, in the safety of the laager—for there were many dangers if they were to go outside, if they were to venture into the open veld.

One afternoon, they were reminded, dreadfully and forcibly, of these dangers.

Laura was sitting under the shade of a tree, with the children around her, and they were doing arithmetic.

'No, Mariette, you did not take the time to think,' Laura said. 'You must surely know by now, that five times seven is not forty-six. Come, try once more.'

But before the child could try again, there was a long and shuddering scream from just outside the camp. The next moment there was a shot. And then silence.

Two of the little girls began to cry, and Laura instinctively drew them close to her.

'Is it the Kaffirs again?' Dirkie asked. 'If it is, I'll help you to load this time, Laura.'

But it was not the Kaffirs.

'Lion,' one of the men told them briefly. 'They've shot him, but I think someone's been hurt.'

Gently, Laura put the children from her.

'If someone is hurt,' she told them steadily, 'we must be ready to help. I'm going to get some water from the fire, and some cloths.' She looked down at them. 'I want you all to stay here, until I come back.'

There was a fire near them, and she found a basin and some cloths, and then, trying to still her thudding heart, she hurried over towards the crowd which had gathered.

The first thing she saw was the lion's body, and although it was well and truly dead, the size of it shook her. True, they had heard the roar of lions in the distance sometimes, but to see one right here, right on the edge of the camp—Then, close to the body, she saw something else. The body of one of the native servants.

'He went to collect wood,' she heard someone say, 'and the lion attacked him.'

'And it would have charged on the camp, then, if Paul hadn't shot it.'

'But it clawed his arm as it fell,' someone else said.

Paul? There were, surely, other men called Paul in their trek?

Perhaps there were, she thought the next moment, but it was Paul Venter who was helped towards her now, his sunbrowned face drained of colour, his arm bleeding. Laura seemed to have been the only person to have thought of bringing water, and immediately a way was cleared for her. She knelt down beside the big fair man as he leaned back against a tree, his eyes closed. Gently, but firmly, she cleaned the blood from his arm, and her heart turned over in relief as she saw that it was little more than a surface wound, although he had lost a considerable amount of blood.

All the time she worked, he lay back, his eyes closed, and although it must have been painful, the near-boiling water on the open wound, she knew she had to do it. There was danger of infection, and he knew too, for he did not flinch. At last it was clean, and she bound it.

'Thank you,' he said, his eyes still closed. 'You are very gentle.'

He opened his eyes.

'So,' he said, without expression, 'I am once again

beholden to you, Miss Conway.' He forced himself to sit up. 'Thank you, I shall do very well now.'

Laura stood up, realising for the first time that his blood was on her dress.

'I am sure you shall, Mr Venter,' she replied, and she lifted her chin high. 'But that dressing must be changed tomorrow. Please do not forget that.'

She turned then, lifted the basin she had used, and went away. When she reached the children, they were all silent, their eyes wide at the sight of her.

'Is someone dead?' one of the boys asked.

Steadily, Laura told them that one of the servants had been killed by a lion, but the lion itself was now dead. And then, with only a moment's hesitation, she turned to Paul's little sister.

'It was your brother who shot the lion, Mariette,' she told her. 'If he hadn't, someone else would undoubtedly have been hurt. He—he has hurt his arm, that is all.' She smiled down at the child. 'Now it will be your turn to look after him.'

'I'll do that, Laura,' Mariette promised earnestly. Laura had long since agreed to the children calling her Laura. 'Because I would like to be able to look after people, when I'm grown up.'

The next morning, before the trek got under way, Paul Venter came to her and asked her if she would change his dressing. Silently, efficiently, she did so, glad to see that already the wound looked clean and healthy. When she had finished he thanked her, courteously. That night, and for the next three mornings and evenings, he came to have his dressing changed. But he took care, Laura thought, to come when he was certain he would not be alone with her. And of course, she told herself, I am very glad indeed of that!

By the time his arm needed no further attention, Laura's entire care was for Stephen's mother, for it was apparent now that she would not live much longer. Laura had not said this to Stephen, but she could see that he knew, and that he had accepted it. As often as he could, as often as his responsibilities to the trek permitted, he came and sat beside his mother, holding her thin hands in his, talking to her cheerfully of days gone by, of things he remembered from his childhood. And Laura, her eyes often blurred with tears, could not help overhearing, could not help being impressed and moved by Stephen's gentle consideration.

One night, she was standing outside their wagon, trying to regain control of herself before she walked through the busy clearing of the encampment, when Stephen came out. Gently, he put his arm around her shoulders, and turned her towards him.

'Tears, Laura?' he asked her. 'For my mother?'

She nodded, for a moment unable to speak.

'And for myself,' she said at last, not quite steadily. 'I—I keep thinking, Stephen, that in many ways I wish I had had the chance to do as much for my father. There was not even the chance to say goodbye, for he was killed in action.'

He held her while she wept, and when her tears were at last over he dried her face gently, and then, his fingers awkward, he tried to make her hair tidy before he took her back to the wagon. He is a good man, a good and kind man, Laura thought again, with gratitude and affection. There are not too many like him.

The herbs that Tante Martha brewed seemed to help the pain that Mrs Smit had, and most of the time she was neither asleep nor awake, but somewhere between the two. There was only once, in those last few days, that she regained consciousness enough to say much. Laura, weary herself, must have closed her eyes, for she woke to find the sick woman's eyes open, and resting on her.

'Not long now, Laura,' Stephen's mother murmured, and there was so much acceptance in her voice and in her face, that Laura knew it would be wrong to attempt to deny this. 'Laura—I have no right to ask you this, but—if you could find it in your heart—Stephen will be so alone.'

And then, before Laura could say anything, Mrs Smit covered her hand with her own thin white one.

'No, my child,' she said, and suddenly her voice was stronger than it had been for days. 'No, Laura, that is quite wrong of me. I have no right to ask any promises of you, and you are to forget what I said.'

But it was not easy to forget, and two days later, when Stephen's mother was dead, and there had been another funeral service and another grave left behind them, Laura knew that although she had made no promise, the thought was growing in her heart that before long she would say yes to Stephen.

Through the weeks and months they had trekked, she had grown more and more conscious of the worth of this quiet, gentle young man. If they had remained on the farm, if they had chosen not to trek, would she have come to know him so well? The through crossed Laura's mind more and more often.

And the same with Tante Martha. All the time Laura had been part of their household at Morgenster, Tante Martha had been kind, but somehow distant. But over the hours they had spent together nursing Stephen's mother, a closeness had grown between them. There were qualities in Tante Martha, Laura had found, that continually surprised her.

It was Tante Martha, now, who insisted that they must celebrate Christmas.

'We left Graaff-Reinet in August,' she said firmly, when they were all gathered around the camp-fire one night in December. 'It is now only a week until Christmas. The time we have trekked has been long, and when I look around I see weariness on many faces. I say we must make camp here, and we must rest until Christmas, and then we must celebrate as well as we may.'

Paul Venter pointed out, pleasantly, that they could not afford to lose a week's trekking. But Tante Martha shook her head.

'There are many repairs needing to be done,' she reminded him. 'You know yourself that much that has been done has been only temporary. The time could be used to good advantage. There is game enough here —we could salt and dry some against the times when we will find none. And more than that, young man. The Lord has protected us for all these weeks and months. He has sustained us through our losses and our troubles. We will observe his birth day fittingly, Paul Venter.'

There was no further argument, and Tante Martha began to organise preparations for Christmas Day. It could be nothing like the Christmas celebrations that had taken place at Morgenster and the other farms left behind, and yet there was a simplicity and a dignity that Laura found strangely moving.

The trekkers rose early on Christmas Day, as they did every day, for the coolness of the early morning was the pleasantest and the most productive part of the day. After the first cup of coffee had been drunk and the rusks eaten, they gathered together around the embers of the camp fire, and there Piet Marais read from the Bible, the Old Testament and then the New.

After that Laura and her small pupils gave a short representation of the coming of the Wise Men to the stable. Mariette, her small face rapt and intent, gazed down at the baby in her arms, and Dirkie, a somewhat fierce Joseph, stood protectively beside her as the Wise Men bearing their gifts knelt in worship.

The hunting party had managed to shoot half a dozen small wild pigs, and throughout the day there was the mouthwatering smell of the pigs roasting. By late afternoon the food was ready, and although it lacked many of the side dishes and accompaniments, there was a feeling of festivity around the camp fire by the time the meal was over.

The children, already grown older than their years in these weeks and months of trekking, neither asked for nor expected any Christmas presents, but Tante Martha had got a party of women together to make tiny dolls from clothes-pegs for the girls, while Stephen and some of the men had made bows and arrows for the boys.

Laura had had little exchange with Paul Venter since there had been no further need to dress his arm. He had not even spoken to her on this day, she thought—and as soon as the thought was there, she was furious with herself, for what did it matter to her what Paul Venter said or did not say. As the sun began to sink, and the day to come to a close, she busied herself with the children, admiring Dirkie's prowess with his bow and arrow, sharing Mariette's pleasure in her tiny peg doll.

'I like her most of all, Laura,' the little girl said earnestly, 'because I can hold her in my hand, and I can carry her with me wherever I go. Is she not the dearest little doll?'

'She is indeed, Mariette,' Laura agreed, and a wave of affection for the child swept over her, so that she bent and hugged Mariette. And it was as she raised her face from the little girl's golden head that she saw Paul Venter standing at the other side of the fire, watching them. He was standing very still, and in the dim firelight she could see no expression on his face. But there was something disturbing, she had to admit, in the very intensity of his stillness.

'It is late, Mariette,' she said, a little breathlessly. 'I—I think perhaps your brother is thinking it is more than time you were in bed. And I must go and help with the washing of the dishes.'

And help she did, with more willingness than usual, relieved to be able to move away from the gaze of the big fair man, but unable to forget how still he had stood, there in the firelight.

Then, a few days later, something happened that put all thoughts of Paul Venter from her mind.

'Laura, where is Dirkie?' Lisbet asked, coming into the wagon where Laura was mending a torn dress.

'He went off to play with the Viljoen boys when we finished school,' Laura told her.

'He is not with them now,' Lisbet said, 'for it was young Gerrit Viljoen who came to me seeking Dirkie.'

Laura stood up.

'I'll look for him', she said. 'He has surely gone to play with someone else, or perhaps to watch the men skinning the game they have killed today.'

But no one had seen Dirkie. The sun set, and suddenly it was dark, and he was still missing. They had searched everywhere, and Lisbet was white-faced, beyond tears. Laura knew that in all of their minds was the memory of the lion, so close to the camp.

Little could be done in the darkness, although Laura and Lisbet, with Stephen helping, went round the edge of the camp with lanterns, calling the child's name, and straining to hear any reply. But there was none. They made no pretence of going to bed, and sat for most of the night close to the fire, getting up only to call his name again.

In the morning, at first light, Paul Venter came to them, his face grim.

'We have found signs of struggling, just outside the laager,' he told them. 'And one of the Hottentot servants is missing.' He hesitated and then, levelly, went on, 'It is impossible to tell what has happened, but it seems to me that Dirkie may have surprised the servant running off, perhaps with things he had stolen. A horse has gone as well. Dirkie may have followed him, and—it may have been easier for him to take the child. He may even have some idea of using him as exchange for further supplies.'

Now Lisbet was crying, silent tears running down her white cheeks.

Paul Venter took both her hands in his.

'We are getting ready now to ride off in search of them, Mrs Conway,' he told her, quietly. 'And—we will do everything in our power to find him.'

He turned then, but before he had gone more than a few steps, Laura ran after him and caught his arm.

'I'm coming too,' she said, breathlessly. 'I can ride as well as any man, and—he is my brother.'

He shook her hand off, and looked down at her.

'Do not make yourself ridiculous, Miss Conway,' he said coldly. 'This is men's work.'

And without waiting for any reply, he strode away.

Mutinously, Laura watched him go. No, she thought, with rising defiance, no, I will not sit here while Dirkie is lost.

A plan began to form in her head. Leaving Lisbet with her mother, she hurried into the wagon. Yes, the kist did have those old clothes that had belonged to Oom Jan when he was younger, slimmer. She pulled a pair of breeches out, and pulled them on over her drawers. They were much too wide, and she took one of her own sashes and tied it firmly around her waist. Now a shirt and a jacket. And, of course a cap, big enough to bundle her hair into. Fortunately, Oom Jan had had a number of hats, and most of them were big enough to take Laura's long but fine brown hair, bundled quickly out of sight.

There was a mirror above the mattress, and she peered into it. At a swift glance—and surely no one would have time to give her more than a swift glance—she would pass for a boy.

A horse was no problem, for she could manage any horse, and she had often ridden astride when there was no one to see. She had a moment's misgiving when she thought of Lisbet's anxiety, so she scribbled a hasty note to tell her what she had done, and left it on the mattress. Then, on the horse that had been Oom Jan's, she rode across to join the group of men, already mounted, being given directions by Paul Venter.

'No one is to ride alone,' he said briefly. 'Parties of at least three or four. We start together, and then we split up.'

Scouts had already followed what there was of a trail, but very soon all traces of any track were lost in the arid veld.

Paul Venter, his hat pushed back on his head, scanned the horizon. Then he turned to Piet Marais.

'You take half the party in that direction, Piet,' he said. 'You others—follow me.'

And Laura, pushing her cap firmly down to hide her hair, and keeping her face averted, found herself galloping across the veld after Paul Venter, in search of her small brother.

CHAPTER
EIGHT

THE vastness of the veld, as the search party fanned out, brought despair to Laura's heart. How could they hope to find Dirkie in this emptiness? No one even knew, for sure, that he had in fact been taken away, willingly or unwillingly, by the servant who had also disappeared.

And yet—surely if he had been attacked by—by a lion, someone of the party would have heard? It could only be that a servant he knew had somehow forced him to keep quiet . . . Desperately, Laura sought to reassure herself, as she galloped across the veld behind Paul Venter—Paul, who had dismissed her plea to join in the search with the contemptuous remark that this was men's work.

Slowly, steadily, the search party moved onward, hoping for some clue, some sign that Dirkie had gone —or been taken—this way. But there was nothing. Paul Venter, at the head of the party, reined in his horse.

'We'll split up further,' he said. 'Two groups, and I will lead one to the right, while Stephen Smit leads the other to the left. We will go on searching until an hour before sundown—then we ride back to camp. At the pace we are moving to search, a fast gallop should take us back. Right—you men on this side, come with me.'

For a moment, it seemed to Laura that his eyes rested on her face, and she moved, hoping that the shadow of the brim of the hat would further hide her. But he said nothing, and Laura, with the four others of the now small party, rode off with him.

Once again, they fanned out, moving slowly. And still there was nothing. Oh Dirkie, Laura thought, and tears blurred her eyes, where are you?

There was a small koppie in line with where she was riding, and at the top she reined in, and shading her eyes against the sun, she looked around. Nothing. Vast miles of nothing, she thought, despairing. And then, far in the distance, near a riverbed, she saw something. Was it a figure on horseback? And—was there a smaller figure, held in front? She strained to see, but it was too far.

Afterwards, she was to blame herself bitterly for acting on impulse, with no thought for what she was doing. But in that moment, the only certainty in her mind was that there was Dirkie, she had found him, she could take him back to Lisbet.

No other member of the party was near her, and although she knew that she should have waited for Paul, and reported to him, she did not do more than glance around. And when she saw that no one was near enough to hear her, she rode off at a gallop, towards the riverbed, without so much as a backward glance.

She was perhaps halfway across the plain that sloped gently down towards the dry riverbed, when she heard thundering hooves behind her. Even as she turned round, Paul Venter was there, one hand on the reins of her horse, pulling her to a halt.

'What the devil do you think you're doing?' he said furiously. 'Didn't you hear my orders?' And then, with sudden suspicion, 'Who are you, anyway?'

Laura said nothing.

He reached out, pulled her hat from her head, and her long brown hair tumbled down over her shoulders.

Defiantly, she kept her chin high, and refused to look away.

'I might have known,' he said, and the cool hostility of his voice chilled her. But only for a moment.

'I had to come,' she told him, rebelliously. 'I couldn't sit there and—and not be out helping to look for Dirkie. And—I saw someone, from the top of the koppie, a figure on horseback, down in the riverbed. I think there is a small figure there too.'

Paul Venter looked at her, his clear blue eyes steady.

'Then why,' he asked her, 'did you not tell me, and let the whole group swing this way? It was only sheer luck that I happened to see you ride off. Do you realise that if anything happened to you, we would have to search for you as well as the boy? Do you know just how irresponsibly you behaved?'

For the first time, Laura did.

'I—I suppose I did,' she said, and now she had to look away. 'But—but I did see them, they're ahead of us, in the dry riverbed. Please—we're halfway there, we must go on.'

For a moment, he hesitated.

'The rest of the party,' he told her, 'will obey my orders, even if I am not there. All right—we will try, but only on the understanding, Miss Conway, that you obey my orders. Without question.'

Laura looked up at him, mutinously.

'I don't see why I should obey—' she began.

His hand tightened on the reins of her horse.

'Otherwise,' he told her, levelly, 'I shall put you across my saddle, and ride right back.'

There was no doubt that he would do it. She knew that.

'All right,' she agreed, knowing she spoke sullenly, and not caring.

They rode towards the riverbed, not as quickly as Laura would have liked to, but at a good steady pace. When they reached the dry, stony bed that looked as if it had not seen water in a hundred years, Paul dismounted.

'But—' Laura began, impatiently.

He looked at her.

She was silent, knowing that this man would not stand for anything but the complete and unquestioning obedience he had demanded.

He bent down, close to the ground.

'Did you say you saw them in the riverbed?' he asked her.

'It looked like that, from the distance,' she replied.

He stood up.

'Someone has undoubtedly ridden up here, very recently,' he said. 'We will do the same—follow me.'

As they set off, riding up the stony and dry riverbed, he glanced at the sky. Laura had not noticed how much it had changed. There were grey and sullen clouds now, and ahead of them it looked even more threatening.

'I do not like this,' Paul Venter said, almost to himself. 'If it does rain, we'll lose all trace of tracks.'

'Then we must hurry,' Laura replied, impatient. 'Before the rain does come.'

'We do not wish to be overheard,' he told her. 'If I am right, if old Klaas has indeed decided to run away, and for some reason has Dirkie with him—he will hide at the first sound of pursuit. So—we will go as I said, steadily, and quietly.'

Laura never knew how long they rode up the dry riverbed in silence. Every so often Paul dismounted and knelt down, and then, seeming satisfied, he rode on.

Then, as he made to mount again, he seemed to stumble, and Laura saw that all the colour had drained from his face.

'What is wrong?' she asked, sharply, frightened by his sudden pallor.

'It is—nothing,' he said, so obviously untruthfully that she dismissed it, and jumping down, ran over to him.

'Now, tell me what is wrong,' she told him.

'My arm hurts,' he admitted, reluctantly.

His arm! She had forgotten, in her anxiety for Dirkie, that his wounded arm was barely healed.

'You had better sit down,' she told him. 'Have you some brandy?'

She took the flask from his pocket, and made him drink some. And then, from her own saddle bag, she took some of the dried strips of meat, called biltong, and gave him some to chew.

'It will do us no harm to rest for a little,' she told him, ashamed of herself for not seeing that he had been in pain.

After a little while, she saw, with relief, that some of the colour had returned to his face. He sat up.

'We can go on now,' he told her brusquely, and she realised that he was humiliated by having to admit his own weakness.

As they mounted and rode on again—and Laura saw that Paul was holding his wounded arm more carefully now—the rain began. Large drops that started slowly, and then began to fall rapidly, until in no time they were both very wet.

Paul reined in.

'I do not like this,' he said, quietly.

'What is a little rain?' Laura replied, although she was

already wet and uncomfortable. 'We must be close to them now.'

'The rain here does not worry me,' he said, with some impatience. 'It is what has fallen already, ahead of us, that makes me uneasy.'

For a moment, he sat still, thinking. Laura, not really understanding what he meant, forced herself to remain silent. And then, with a shrug, he rode on again, and she followed.

For some time, they rode on through the rain, steadily. Then, once again, Paul Venter reined in. This time, he dismounted, and stood very still. But not for long. Suddenly he swung back to Laura.

'Get out of this riverbed,' he told her, tersely. 'Quick —off your horse and lead him, and get out—fast!'

There was something in his face and in his voice that made Laura realise that this was no time to argue. She did as he told her, dismounted, and led the horse up the steep riverbank, until they were high above the riverbed, looking down at it.

'Farther,' Paul Venter ordered, and they led the horses—both suddenly and inexplicably terrified—still higher. Then Paul stopped.

'What is it?' Laura began to ask, but even as she spoke, she heard a dull, distant roar.

'Thunder?' she said, but Paul shook his head.

'Water,' he told her. 'The river in flood.'

The next moment, as they watched, it came. A wall of water six feet high, surging along what had moments ago been a dry and empty riverbed. In seconds, the part where they had been riding was under water, and Laura realised, with sickening fear, that they would have been swept away completely, horses and all. And as she realised that, there was another thought.

She turned to Paul, stricken. Somehow it did not even surprise her that he knew immediately what she was thinking.

'If it is indeed Dirkie ahead of us, with old Klaas,' he said carefully, 'they would also hear the water. An old Hottentot like Klaas knows the danger with a cloudburst like this, he would have them on high ground, in safety. But—Laura, we can do nothing more, now, until the water goes down. We must look for shelter.'

More shaken than she had realised, Laura followed him to higher ground. There he found a cave—not a deep one, but enough to afford them shelter, so that their horses could stand well out of the rain, and they themselves could retreat deeper.

'If we could see, I am certain there would be Bushman paintings,' Paul said, looking around. 'This is just the sort of cave they liked.'

But already it was darker, not only because it was growing late, but because of the low and threatening clouds.

'What are we going to do?' Laura asked, not quite steadily.

He shrugged.

'We have little choice,' he told her. 'We must remain here until daylight. And then—well, then we must see if the river is down.'

'All night?' Laura asked.

'There is nothing else we can do,' he told her, somewhat impatiently.

He made her drink some of his brandy, and they both ate some more biltong. He tied the horses' reins around a piece of rock, although both horses were too much afraid to move.

It was almost dark now, but she could see him look down at her.

'You had better take off that wet jacket,' he said, and he took off his own. 'For myself, I do not intend to catch a severe chill by remaining in soaking clothes, and I shall remove my outer clothing. I suggest that you do the same, Miss Conway.'

Laura was glad that the growing darkness hid the warm colour in her cheeks.

'I cannot do that, Mr Venter,' she pointed out. 'Not when you and I are—are alone in this cave.'

She heard him sigh.

'May I remind you,' he said coolly, 'that it is your own foolish behaviour that has brought us both here. We must make the best of it now. I shall remain in this corner, and you may go over there, and I shall then endeavour to forget that you are sitting there in your drawers and chemise! Now for heaven's sake, Miss Conway, be sensible.'

Laura would not have thought it possible that her cheeks could grow even hotter.

'There is no need to be vulgar, Mr Venter,' she told him. And then, in her own dark little corner, she proceeded to do as he had suggested, and she had to admit that it was a relief to be out of the wet trousers and shirt, which she spread out, along with the jacket, to try to dry.

The ground itself was hard, and the wall of the cave cold, but at least, she told herself, they were dry now, for she could hear the rain falling steadily outside.

I shall sleep, she told herself, and when I wake, we can go on and search for Dirkie, and by nightfall tomorrow we can be back at the camp. She refused to allow herself to think of the other possibilities—that it might not be Dirkie ahead of them with old Klaas, that even if it was, they might not have escaped the flood of water in the riverbed. That—

No, I shall sleep, Laura told herself again, even more firmly.

But sleep was far from easy, in the cold and in the dark. Then something brushed her face, and she gave a gasp.

'What is it?' Paul Venter's voice asked, from the darkness.

'I don't know,' Laura replied. 'Something touched my face.'

She heard him sigh.

'Only a bat,' he told her.

'A bat?'

And in the same instant, it brushed against her cheek again, soft and feathery and terrifying. This time Laura screamed, and with no conscious thought, stumbled across the darkness of the cave until she almost fell over Paul Venter.

'Steady,' he said, and incredibly there was laughter in his voice.

Laura burst into tears, tears brought on by the worry and the stress, by the danger they had so recently escaped, and now, by him laughing because she was terrified of bats.

'Laura, don't cry,' he said then, awkwardly. In the darkness, his arm came around her. 'I can't even see you—where is your face, girl? Look, I haven't even a handkerchief, for heaven's sake don't cry!'

Somehow, the warmth and the reassurance of his arm around her stilled the growing panic in Laura, and she managed to stop crying.

'I'm—sorry,' she said at last, with difficulty. And then, because it had to be said, 'I'm sorry most of all that

I was so foolish, coming away by myself, so that you had to come after me.'

'Never mind,' he replied, and she realised that the coolness and the hostility had gone from his voice. 'You have been very brave, you're entitled to cry if you want to.'

'I don't, any more,' Laura told him, surprised to find that this was true.

And then, suddenly, realisation came. Here she was, in the darkness of this cave, alone with this man, and she wearing only her chemise and her drawers. And she had no idea how much, or how little, he was wearing.

'I—I had better—' she began, uncertainly.

'Laura,' he said, and there was something in the lazy warmth of his voice when he said her name, that made her heart thud unevenly against her ribs. 'Laura, stay here.'

In the darkness, his lips found hers, and he kissed her, gently at first. She was lost. Her limbs had turned to water, and the blood surged in her veins. She could not have moved, even if she had wanted to. And then his lips became more insistent, more demanding, and in a confusion and a tumult of strange feelings, her body was responding to his, as she clung to him.

Then, slowly, his lips left hers, and he drew back from her.

Laura, bewildered, shaken, would have clung to him again, but his hands on her shoulders held her off.

'I think,' he said, not quite steadily, 'you had better go back to the other side. The bats are of less danger to you than I am.'

'But—but Paul—' Laura murmured, unable to think clearly, wanting only to go back into his arms. 'Paul—'

'Listen to me, Laura, and do as I say!' he told her,

almost angrily. 'Or you stay here, and I will move!'

Which he did, leaving her leaning against the wall of the cave, her heart gradually returning to its normal speed. For a long time, she sat there, and then, slowly, complete understanding came to her. She wanted to speak to him, to thank him for drawing them both back to their senses. For he could so easily, she admitted to herself with honesty, have done anything he wished with her. She had been in no state to stop him. In fact, she had not wanted him to stop at all.

The honesty of that admission changed things completely. In the darkness, Laura smiled. So the hard-hearted and arrogant Paul had a different side, a noble and a chivalrous side that she had never suspected. He could have taken advantage of her completely, and he had not.

In the morning, Laura thought, drowsily, I shall tell him how grateful I am to him. And I think, somehow, that things may well be different, from now on, between Paul Venter and me.

She slept, then, somewhat to her own surprise. When she woke, there was no sound of rain, and already there was enough light to see the horses in the doorway of the cave, and Paul, still asleep in the corner opposite her. He looked, she thought with tenderness, curiously defence-less asleep. She wanted to touch his sunbleached hair gently, as she had done that night when little Mariette was so ill. But she knew, because of last night, that she must not, that she must stay where she was.

Her clothes were almost dry, and she pulled on the trousers and the shirt again, and tied the trousers with her sash. She had just finished buttoning the shirt, when she saw Paul open his eyes.

For a moment he looked at her, uncomprehending,

and then, as she watched, she saw that he was re-membering. A flood of warm colour stained her cheeks.

'Paul,' she said, not quite steadily. 'I—I want to thank you.'

He looked at her, and now she saw, dismayed, that the warmth was gone from his eyes and his face.

'I did some thinking,' he told her, his voice level, 'last night, and I have come to this conclusion. Since every-one will naturally assume the worst about this night spent here alone, you had better marry me.'

She could not believe she had heard him aright. Not only his words, but the cool and hostile way he had said them.

'What do you mean?' she said, bewildered.

He shrugged.

'You must know very well, Laura,' he said impa-tiently, 'that no one is likely to believe that you and I spent a night here alone in all innocence. That is why I say you had better marry me, and still the talk.

Laura thought that she had never felt so cold. Not even when she was soaked in the cloudburst yesterday. And then, slowly, anger rose in her. She lifted her head and looked at the big fair man.

'I certainly will not marry you,' she said to him, hoping her voice was cool enough and steady enough to hide the bewilderment and the hurt she felt. 'I have no need of your charity, Paul Venter, in any way at all!'

CHAPTER
NINE

THERE was only the distance of the cave between them,
yet it seemed to Laura a gulf that could never be bridged,
because of what Paul Venter had said. And the way he
had said it.

'Very well,' he said, after a moment, and his voice was
indifferent. But Laura was now beyond being hurt by
him. 'If that is the way you want it. The talk and the
gossip—for there will be that, in plenty, make no mis-
take—will not worry you?'

'Will it worry you?' she flashed back at him, glad of the
sustaining power of her anger.

'It is always different for a man,' he replied, and the
undoubted truth of that—unpalatable as it was—could
not be denied.

'I would prefer to regard the matter as closed,' Laura
said, and somehow she managed to keep her voice
steady. 'The rain has stopped—what do you intend that
we do?'

For answer he pulled his outer clothes towards him.
Laura turned away sharply, and when he joined her at
the mouth of the cave, he was fully dressed. Without a
word, he strode past her.

'Where—where are you going?' Laura asked, furious
with herself at the stab of fear that she knew he must
hear in her voice.

'To see the river, and judge if we can proceed. Wait there,' he told her peremptorily.

Laura waited. And as she waited, she told herself that the only thing that mattered was finding Dirkie. What people might say—what had happened last night between Paul Venter and herself—the way he had spoken to her this morning—none of this was important. Only finding Dirkie.

'The river is considerably down,' Paul Venter said, as he came near the cave. 'We can ride by the side of it, but—'

'But what?' Laura asked him, levelly.

He hesitated, but only for a moment.

'We are not certain that Dirkie and old Klaas are ahead of us,' he reminded her. 'And—even if it was them that you saw, there is no telling what has happened during this flash flood.'

Laura felt all the colour drain from her face. It was something that she had had to think of, but to hear it put brutally into words like that was almost too much for her. And yet, afterwards, she had to admit that perhaps it was better to bring the possibility into the open.

'Then if it is possible, I should want to know what has happened,' she said, as steadily as possible. 'Can we start now?'

For a moment, she saw unwilling admiration in his eyes. Then there was nothing but the cool hostility she had come to know so well.

They could not ride in the riverbed, as they had done before the flash flood, but they managed to ride as near as possible on the bank. All the time they rode, they watched the river, now sluggish where it had flowed so swiftly and dangerously in the dry bed the day before. But there was nothing and no one to be seen, and Laura knew that it could not be long before Paul Venter decided that they must go back to the camp—where they could well, she knew, have been given up for lost.

'Stop!' the big fair man in front of her said suddenly, and Laura reined in her horse immediately. She could neither see nor hear anything, but she remained silent, watching Paul Venter turn his head from side to side, slowly.

'There is smoke somewhere near,' he said tersely. 'I cannot see it, but I can smell it. Dismount, and tie your horse to this tree, beside mine. Now, we will move on foot, but you must do exactly as I tell you, for there is no telling who it could be ahead of us.'

Round the next corner, they both saw at the same time a thin wisp of smoke. Soundlessly, Paul Venter moved forward, and Laura, glad of the ease of movement provided by the trousers she was wearing, followed him. And there, on the riverbank, was the old Hottentot servant, with Dirkie beside him. Dirkie, with dark shadows and tear-stains on his small face, but safe, and alive.

It was only Paul Venter's hand on her arm that stopped Laura from running out from the shelter of the trees, and taking her small brother in her arms.

'Wait,' he whispered.

The old man was bending over the small fire, and now, as they watched, he urged the child closer to it. Dirkie did not seem to be afraid of him, Laura realised.

'Klaas,' Paul Venter said clearly, and drawing Laura with him, he walked out towards the old man and the boy.

'Laura?' Dirkie said, as if he could hardly believe it, and the next moment he hurtled himself towards her. Her arms closed around him, and they were both crying.

'Oh Laura,' Dirkie sobbed. 'I thought I would never see Mother or you or Ouma again! And I was so frightened when the river came, and I would have fallen into the water, but Klaas pulled me out, and we hided up here until the rain stopped.'

Laura held him close, asking no questions, until at last he was calm. When he was silent, Paul Venter, who had been questioning the old servant rapidly, in his own tongue, turned to her.

'Klaas had had enough of trekking,' he told her. 'He stole some food and some ammunition, and he left. He thought that either he'd find some of his own people, or he would come on a place where trekkers had decided to settle. But Dirkie saw him stealing the horse, and I think the old man panicked. He grabbed Dirkie, and took him with him, meaning to set him free a little way from the camp, so that he could make his way back. But they saw a lion, and Klaas couldn't leave Dirkie, so—he had to take him with him. Then the flash flood came, and I gather Dirkie might have been swept away if the old man hadn't saved him.' He looked down at the boy. 'Is that right, Dirkie?'

Dirkie nodded.

'I didn't mean to be naughty,' he said, and now his voice shook. 'Is—is everyone very angry? It was just —when I saw Klaas taking Oom Piet's horse, I wanted to stop him.'

Paul Venter knelt down, and took the child's hands in his.

'No one is angry with you, Dirkie,' he said, and the unexpected gentleness of his voice unnerved Laura. 'But everyone is terribly worried, so the sooner we get back the better. You can ride with me, and Klaas can ride Oom Piet's horse.' He turned to Laura. 'He's had enough of escaping,' he told her. 'He wants to come back. I think he's been punished enough.'

'And he did save Dirkie's life,' Laura agreed.

Paul Venter lifted Dirkie on to his big black horse, and mounted himself, and the small procession began to make its way back along the riverbank, and then across the plain, up to the koppie from where Laura had seen the figures in the riverbed, and then back towards the camp.

It was afternoon before they reached it, and in the vast emptiness of the veld they must have been seen from a considerable distance. Everyone, it seemed to Laura, was gathered beside the wagons, waiting for them. The men, obviously returned from searching again, and the women and children.

Laura's eyes searched for her stepmother. Lisbet was standing at the back, and her face was white and still. As if, Laura thought, she dare not let herself believe that they were back safely, until they were close to her. Piet Marais was beside her, and Laura, with a pang, saw that Lisbet turned to him, seeking reassurance. But when the farmer replied to her, there was kindess and gentleness on his face. Laura thought, afterwards, that it was in that moment that she really accepted that her stepmother might marry again.

'Dirkie!' Lisbet said, and now she came forward. Paul Venter swung himself down from his horse, and then handed the child to his mother. For a moment, Lisbet held him close to her, and tears ran down her cheeks. Then she turned and held out one hand to Laura, and Laura, all at once uncertain of her reception, ran to her stepmother.

She drew back, at last, from the welcoming clasp of Lisbet's arms, as Paul Venter finished the story of how the old servant Klaas had unwillingly taken Dirkie with him, and had later saved his life in the flash flood.

'Klaas is back, and he does not wish to leave the trek again,' Paul finished, quietly. 'And I for one feel that no further punishment is necessary. I am certain he will be a good and faithful servant from now on.'

There was a moment of hesitation, and then the other men nodded in agreement.

'And so you found Klaas and the boy, and the four of you then had to shelter from the storm and the flash flood?' someone asked.

For a moment, Paul Venter's eyes met Laura's. It would be easier, she realised immediately, if this was the story that was given. But almost imperceptibly, the big fair man shook his head. And Laura knew that he had weighed up the possibility of letting this be accepted, and had decided that it was not possible. For both Dirkie and the old man might well say something that would let the truth be known. And then it would look worse, that they had tried to conceal it.

'No,' Paul Venter replied, steadily. 'No, we found them only this morning. The flash flood forced Miss Conway and myself to take shelter, and we could only resume our search this morning.'

Laura forced herself to keep her head held high, but she knew that there was a tide of colour in her cheeks as so many heads turned to look from her to Paul Venter, speculatively. Paul, as if unconscious of this, began to discuss the arrangements to be made so that the party could trek at first light the next day.

'Come, Laura and Dirkie,' Lisbet said, and her clear, sweet voice was somehow a rebuke, so that the heads turned away again. 'You are both tired, and extremely dirty.'

She led them back to the wagon, but just as they

reached it, Stephen Smit appeared. Without a word, he took both Laura's hands in his.

'I am—glad you are safe, Laura,' he said, unsteadily. 'I would have continued the search for you in the night, but—it was impossible.' For a long time, it seemed to Laura, his dark eyes searched her face, and when he spoke again, there was a quiet determination in his voice that she had not heard before. 'When you are rested, Laura, I want to talk to you.'

He turned then and left them, and Laura followed Lisbet into the wagon.

Swiftly, her hands tender on the small boy's firm little body, Lisbet washed her son and dressed him again, and sent him outside into the late afternoon sunshine with his grandmother, waiting outside. Then she asked a servant to bring some more hot water, and she stayed with Laura while she also washed. It was only when Laura was once again dressed in a cotton dress, and her hair drawn back neatly, that she knew the moment for speaking could be put off no longer.

'I—should not have done as I did,' she said, uneasily. 'But Lisbet, I could not sit here while Dirkie was lost, I had to be out, helping to search for him. And—and I was the one who saw them, too.' Still her stepmother said nothing. 'I did leave you a note to tell you what I had done,' Laura offered.

Lisbet nodded, and Laura, contrite, saw that she was close to tears.

'I know you did, and I know too that if it had not been for you, Dirkie might not have been found,' she said shakily, 'but—oh, Laura, for all of last night when you did not come back with the search party. I thought I had lost both of you. Piet said I must not give up hope, but it was not easy.'

Piet. Piet Marais. Laura thought of the kindness on his face as he looked down at her stepmother.

'He is a good man, Piet Marais,' she said, steadily, and the gratitude in Lisbet's eyes made her glad she had said it.

'Come, Laura, you must be hungry, let us see if the food is ready,' Lisbet said then.

She had not said a word about the night Laura had spent with Paul Venter taking shelter from the storm and from the river. And Laura, knowing her stepmother as she did, doubted if she ever would. Tears blurred her eyes, for all at once she knew it would have been more than she could bear to be questioned in any way about the time in the cave.

When she went out of the wagon, Stephen was waiting. Lisbet hesitated, her eyes meeting Laura's.

'I wish to talk to Laura, Lisbet,' Stephen told his cousin quietly, firmly. You need not worry, I shall not distress her.'

Still Lisbet hesitated.

'Laura is hungry, and tired,' she said.

Stephen smiled, and the gentle kindness of his smile brought an unexpected tightness to Laura's throat.

'It's all right, Lisbet,' he said. 'Come, Laura.'

Already Laura could feel waves of weariness washing over her. But there was something safe and soothing about Stephen's arm around her shoulders, and she allowed him to lead her a little way from the wagon.

'Now, Laura,' he said to her, and there was quiet certainty in his voice, 'if you will give me permission, I wish to let it be known that you and I are to be married, and that this has been decided between us in secret, for some time.'

Laura looked at him, and the steadfastness of his love

for her, the unquestioning acceptance, made her eyes blur with tears. In spite of herself, she could not help but contrast this with the way Paul Venter had spoken to her this morning. This morning? Was it only this morning? And was last night, in the cave, so recent? In this moment, it seemed to her that it had happened a lifetime ago.

'You would ask me to marry you?' she said shakily. 'Now, Stephen? When—when we know there is likely to be talk?'

'Talk matters nothing to me, Laura,' he told her, and she saw, with wonder, that he meant this. 'And—once it is known that we have been betrothed for some time, there will be less talk. Come, Laura, you have nothing to do but to say yes.' He took something from his pocket. 'See, my mother gave me her betrothal ring before she died. She—hoped that before long, you would be wearing it.'

Why should I not say yes, Laura thought, wearily. Why should I not rest in the haven of Stephen's love?

She hesitated, but only for a moment, for Stephen's dark eyes were warm and loving. He was a good man, Laura told herself, and he loved her. She would be safe, and cared for, with him.

'If you wish me to, then—I will marry you, Stephen,' she said, her voice low.

For a moment, there was such a blaze of joy on his face that she was almost afraid. And then he bent his head, and with his big brown hands all at once clumsy and awkward, he put the small ring of garnets and pearls on the third finger of her left hand.

'Come,' he said, 'and we will tell everyone.'

'Wait, Stephen,' Laura said, for she knew that it had to be said. He looked down at her, waiting. 'I want you to know,' she said, steadily, 'that nothing happened between Paul Venter and me to make me unfit to be your wife.'

For you cannot, she thought, painfully, count something that did not happen.

Stephen kissed her, his lips gentle on hers.

'There was no need to say that, Laura,' he told her. 'But—I thank you.'

He led her to the big camp fire, and Laura could not help but be conscious of the speculation on so many of the faces as she came near.

Stephen, with her hand held in his, so that she could not have escaped even if she had wished to, led her directly to Paul Venter. Laura had not expected this, and for all her resolution, her breath caught in her throat when they reached him.

'I wish to thank you, Paul, for looking after my betrothed so well,' Stephen said, and he looked down at Laura and smiled. 'We have been betrothed for some time, but because of my mother's death, we said nothing. Now, with Laura safely back, I can keep silent no longer. And—I wish you to know how grateful I am to you, Paul.'

For one endless moment, it seemed to Laura, Paul Venter's clear blue eyes sought hers. And she knew that he had guessed the truth, that he knew that this betrothal had only just now happened. Then he looked at Stephen, and there was reluctant admiration on his face.

'But of course, Stephen,' he returned, easily, 'knowing that Laura was your intended, I doubled my efforts to see that she was safe.'

He nodded, then, and turned back to the man he had been talking to. And so, Laura thought, between the man who loved her and the man who could barely stand the sight of her, the talk had been stilled, to a large extent.

Not entirely, of course, she found in the ensuing days. Aletta, in particular, made so many references to the time Laura had spent with Paul Venter, waiting for the river to go down, that both Lisbet and Tante Martha were forced to speak sharply to her.

She also expressed, more than once, her doubts about the time Stephen and Laura had been betrothed.

'It seems very strange to me,' she said, suspiciously, 'that not even your own family knew, Laura.'

'It seemed better that way,' Laura replied, unwilling to lie, but knowing that because of what Stephen had done for her, she must go along with the pretence.

Aletta shrugged.

'Well, I wish you joy of him,' she said. And then, making no attempt to hide the malice she felt—'And I wish him joy of you!'

In the following days, as the trek resumed its steady progress, Laura saw nothing of Paul Venter, except in the distance. But Stephen told her one night, that Paul had spoken to him.

'What did he say?' Laura asked, and she hoped that she sounded unconcerned.

Stephen took her hand in his.

'He told me,' he said, quietly, 'just what you did. That nothing that happened during the time the two of you were alone need cause me any concern.'

No, indeed, thought Laura, with a bitterness that shook her in its intensity. For it certainly did not cause Paul himself any concern.

'What did you reply to him?' she asked, for Stephen was looking down at her, waiting.

'I thanked him,' he said, 'but I told him that it was not necessary for him to say anything at all.' He paused, and then, a little uncertainly, went on, 'Laura, our scouts tell us that Retief's party is only a little ahead of us, and we should catch up with them soon. I hear that there is a predikant travelling with them. We could be married by him.'

'So soon?' Laura said, and the moment she said it, she wished that she could have bitten out her tongue, as she saw the immediate clouding of Stephen's dark eyes. 'I mean—I had not expected that we should be lucky enough to find a predikant this soon.'

'So—when we reach them, I may ask the predikant to marry us?' Stephen asked.

'Of course,' Laura replied, and to still the sudden doubts, she stood on tiptoe and kissed him. 'Of course, Stephen—just as soon as possible.'

The next day, there was word that Piet Retief wished to speak to the leaders of their party, and suggested that they should ride on ahead, for it would be some days before the trek itself could hope to reach the place where Retief's party were encamped. Stephen was to ride with Paul Venter and one or two of the other men, and he would, he said, speak to the predikant.

But before the party left, Paul Venter sought Laura out, among her pupils, and asked her if he could talk to her. Laura at first said she was busy with the children, but he suggested, impatiently, that she set them some task for a few moments. With reluctance, Laura did this, but only because she could see that he was determined to talk to her. She joined him, but insisted on remaining fairly close to the small group of children.

'What can you have to say to me?' she asked him, knowing that she sounded uncivil and not caring.

He took his hat off, and stood with it in his hands, the sun shining on his blond head.

'I must apologise to you,' he said, and this was so unexpected that Laura was at a loss for any reply. In any case, he seemed determined to go on without even waiting. 'Until I met you, I have not known any of the English other than by their deeds. And for their deeds, for what they have done to my people, I have hated them. I have grown up hating them, and nothing I have learned since I became a man has changed my mind. And that is why, Laura, I do not know how to deal with you.'

Laura put out one hand, wanting him to stop, knowing, blindly, that it would be better for both of them if he did. But he seemed determined to say what he had set out to say.

'On the one hand, I want to go on hating the English, feeling I can never trust them, wanting nothing further to do with anyone English. Why should I stop hating them now, and why should I allow myself to trust any one of them? But—on the other hand, I have grown to admire you. You are brave, and you are fearless, and you are spirited. But you are also kind, and—this I will never forget, as well as that—you are lovely, Laura.'

His clear blue eyes met hers, and now they were clouded with bewilderment.

'But at the same time as all that—you are and you always will be English. Your father was an English Captain. And so—and so, that night in the cave, when the only thing in the world I wanted to do was to take you in my arms and keep you there, I—sent you away, and I spoke to you as I did.' He smiled then, but it was a smile with nothing but bitterness in it. 'And—if you had agreed to marry me, I could have told myself that the only reason I did it was for your good name.'

Laura managed to speak.

'Why do you tell me this now, Paul?' she asked him unsteadily.

He shrugged.

'I do not know,' he admitted. And then, with sudden violence that made her breath catch in her throat. 'Yes, by God, I do know. It is because I hear that if there is a predikant with Retief, you and Stephen Smit are to marry. And—'

He stopped.

For a moment, Laura closed her eyes, and tried to still the uneven thudding of her heart.

'You know very well that I am promised to Stephen,' she said, at last.

'I know,' he replied, and there was acceptance in his voice. And then, painfully, 'I only—wanted you to understand, Laura.'

For a moment longer he stood there, looking down at her. But Laura knew that she could say nothing more to him. After a moment she turned and went back to the waiting children.

When she looked back, Paul Venter was still standing there, his hat in his hands, watching her.

CHAPTER
TEN

IT was some time before the men who had gone to meet and talk with Piet Retief at Thaba Nchu returned to the camp.

Many times, in the waiting days and then weeks, Laura was to think of what Paul Venter had said to her, and to remember how he had stood, his hat in his hand, the sunlight on his fair head, watching her.

She knew how hard it must have been, for a man like him, to apologise to her. And in some strange way she found that she could almost begin to understand the confusion of feelings that made him behave as he had to her. But it changed nothing. She knew that, and so did he, and indeed there had been neither opportunity nor need for any further words between them. She had given her promise to Stephen, she was betrothed to him. He had stood by her with strength and steadfastness when she needed him most.

Not that there had been any mention of any change in that, Laura would remind herself hastily when her thoughts took her thus far. Indeed, Paul Venter had made a point of saying to her that all he wanted was that she should understand.

Once or twice, in those waiting weeks Lisbet asked her, with some concern, if she was certain that she was happy to be marrying Stephen.

'There is no finer man than Stephen,' Laura said,

meaning it with all her heart. 'He is kind, and he is gentle, and—he will make a good husband.'

Lisbet's dark eyes held hers, so that Laura could not look away.

'That is not what I asked you,' she pointed out, gently, and Laura's cheeks grew warm. 'I had the feeling, some time back,' Lisbet went on carefully, 'that although you are certainly conscious of all these good qualities in Stephen, yet—you did not think of him as the man you wished to spend the rest of your life with.'

Now Laura looked away.

'I think most young girls dream of—of an unknown man, who will sweep them off their feet, and make life thrilling and exciting,' she said, her voice low, 'but I think too that as girls grow up, they leave these dreams behind, and— they look for a man like Stephen.' She lifted her head, and smiled into her stepmother's concerned face. 'No, Lisbet, you need not worry. I am happy to be marrying Stephen, and we will have a good marriage.'

She was grateful that Lisbet said no more, for now that her mind was made up and she was promised to Stephen, she did not want to talk about it. She was determined that she would think no more about Paul Venter. But often, in the still of the night, she would wake, and she would remember that moment in the cave, when she had been in his arms, with his lips on hers. And in the darkness her cheeks would grow warm with shame, and she would tell herself that the sooner she and Stephen were married the better, and these wayward thoughts of Paul Venter would cease.

In those waiting weeks, while Paul and Stephen and the other two men were with Retief, there was much to be thought of at the camp. There was an increasing danger of attacks from neighbouring tribes, and Paul had insisted, when he left, that they must live under laager conditions, that only the hunting party should leave the safety of the defended wagons. Twice, they were brought news of attacks on other camps, by exhausted riders who were warning any party they knew to be in the vicinity. Each time, they increased the safety precautions, and doubled the watch during the night. There was no attack, but nerves grew strained, and there was tension on every face.

Somewhat to Laura's surprise, Aletta said little more about her betrothal to Stephen. Indeed, she said little to any of them, for she had struck up a friendship with a girl a little younger than herself, one of the Viljoens, and she spent a considerable amount of time with her. Laura and Lisbet too, she knew, although neither of them said anything, were relieved that she seemed to have found a friend, and thus appeared more content.

News was brought to them, when everyone was becoming increasingly concerned, that the men of their party had left Thaba Nchu and gone with Piet Retief to the Zulu Chief Dingaan's capital at Umgungundhlovu, and there was word of a grant of land that might be made around Port Natal. And when, after some weeks, Paul Venter, Stephen Smit and the other two men returned, they confirmed this. But Laura, standing on the outskirts of the group listening to the men talking, had the growing certainty that Paul Venter was not entirely happy about this.

She turned to Stephen, standing with his arm around her.

'What did you think of this Dingaan, Stephen?' she asked him. 'Is he indeed trustworthy—does he mean to do as he says, and grant us land if Mr Retief can procure the return of his stolen cattle for him? Land in a place such as we hear of, seems too good an exchange.'

Stephen shrugged.

'He places great store by these cattle,' he pointed out. 'And as for the land, there is enough and to spare. It is green and fertile, and so beautiful that you will love it. As soon as the settlement is made, we will all move down, and we will be given our own share of the land, and then, Laura, we will establish our own farm.' His dark eyes clouded. 'But as for the predikant, I am afraid we must wait, for our party is not to join the others until Retief has concluded his negotiations with Dingaan. As soon as it is possible, after that, we will be married.'

Laura, listening, was ashamed of the surge of relief she felt when he said this.

To cover her disturbance, she asked him about the Zulu Chief and his capital, and often, in the next few days, she and Dirkie listened, enthralled, to Stephen's description of the huge oval kraal, surrounded by a thorn fence. Hundreds of huts shaped like beehives, and at the top the huts where the Zulu Chief kept his women.

'Hundreds of them, they say,' Stephen told Laura, his voice low. But Dirkie was more interested in the Zulu warriors.

'Thousands of warriors, Stephen?' he asked eagerly.

Stephen smiled.

'Perhaps two thousand, Dirkie,' he replied. 'And all of them completely naked. And Dingaan himself is like polished jet, for they say he is rubbed with grease every day. A big man, he is.'

'But his eyes are small, and there is something in them that I distrust,' Paul Venter said, coming up beside them where they sat beside the camp fire.

Stephen looked up at him.

'Come, Paul, you heard the interpreter tell us of his friendly intentions. Why, if he had meant us harm, he had only to raise his hand, and those warriors would have fallen on us. You know that Piet Retief trusts him completely.'

Paul Venter nodded.

'I know that,' he agreed. 'But Retief is a man who trusts easily. Too easily, perhaps.'

Laura stood up. This was the first time Paul Venter had been near her since the party came back, and she was shaken to find how much it disturbed her.

Stephen stood up as well.

'Perhaps you mistrust too easily, Paul,' he commented. 'When I hear of the worry there has been here lest we were attacked, and when I think of that green and fertile land, and hardly any Zulus until beyond the Tugela—why, man, we would be foolish indeed to refuse this sort of opportunity. Do you ride with Retief when he goes back?'

'He has asked me to,' Paul Venter replied. And then, with an effort obvious to Laura, he brought his thoughts back, looked down at Dirkie, and smiled. 'Well, young Dirkie, I hear from Mariette that you are top of the class with your numbers, but she maintains that when it comes to reading, she is better than you are.'

'She is not!' Dirkie cried indignantly. 'I'm much better than Mariette, am I not, Laura?'

Laura smiled too, glad to talk of other things, for she found it most disturbing that Paul did not feel happy about the proposed settlement.

'Mariette is very good at reading, Dirkie, you must admit that. But she is right to say that your numbers are better.'

'How does she do with her lessons, Miss Conway?'

Paul Venter said, and now he spoke formally. But not, Laura thought, for any reason other than that she was betrothed to another man. The old coolness and hostility were there no longer.

'She is doing very well,' she told him. 'She is eager to learn, and she does her homework. You—you must come by our little class some day, and she will read to you.'

'I should like to do that,' the big fair man replied.

But that night the camp was attacked, and there would be no school for many days. The attacking natives were more numerous than in the previous attack, and more determined, it seemed to Laura, for as fast as one wave was repelled, another was there, flinging themselves against the thorn barrier, and sometimes breaking through the interlocked wagons. There was no time even to be afraid, no time for anything but the constant re-loading as she kept Stephen supplied with a ready gun.

On and on, through the hours of darkness, the attack lasted. Sometimes it seemed to Laura like a nightmare from which she would never wake. There were screams, but she could not tell whether they came from the attacking Kaffirs, or from some member of their party who had been wounded.

At last, with the first light of dawn, it seemed that they had held fast, that the band of attacking natives were withdrawing. Then, suddenly, with a mighty yell, a huge black man leaped through the thorn barrier and was almost on their wagon. Laura was never certain how it happened, but the next moment Stephen was on the ground grappling with the native, she herself held his gun in her hand, knowing that she dare not fire for fear of hitting Stephen.

In the growing light, there was a flash of metal, and Stephen fell. Laura took aim at the black man as he launched himself towards the wagon, but before she could fire, there was a shot from the next wagon, and he fell. Without conscious thought, Laura threw down the gun she was holding and began to scramble down to where Stephen lay. But Paul Venter's hand on her arm, so hard that he almost flung her down, stopped her.

'Stay where you are,' he said tersely. 'There are still plenty of them waiting their chance.'

Laura struggled free.

'But Stephen—' she began.

'You can do nothing for him at this moment,' he told her, levelly. 'If he is dead, there is no need for another life to be lost. And if he is alive, a few moments more will make little difference.'

It seemed to Laura an eternity that they stood there, she rubbing her arm where Paul Venter had bruised it, and he standing still, intent, watching as it became lighter, in case any more of the attackers remained.

'I shall go,' he told her, at last, and he jumped down to where Stephen lay. Laura watched as he knelt beside him.

'He is alive,' he said, after a moment. 'But he is badly wounded. Laura, go and fetch Piet Marais, for we must lift Stephen with great care.'

The two men carried Stephen, unconscious and bleeding badly from a wound in his back, just below his waist, and laid him down inside the wagon, where Laura and Tante Martha were soon ready with boiling water. For all that Laura had had some experience of nursing in the past few months, she had to close her eyes for a moment when she saw the blood.

'He—has lost a great deal of blood, Tante Martha,' she said, unsteadily, and the old woman, intent on cleaning the wound, nodded.

'He has, Laura,' she agreed. 'But—I do not think the loss of blood is the bad thing, for Stephen. It is the position of the wound itself that concerns me, so close to the spine. I fear—'

She said no more then, and it was only later that Laura remembered her words, remembered the expression on her face as she bent over her nephew. And in the days that followed, as all through the camp people tended their wounded, and buried their dead, she did not again say as much.

Stephen remained unconscious for some time, and then lay, gradually regaining his understanding and his realisation as some strength returned to him. Laura and Tante Martha between them nursed him.

It was on the fourth day after the attack, that Laura, sitting drowsing beside her patient, opened her eyes to find Stephen, for the first time fully conscious, watching her.

'Stephen!' she said, joyfully. 'You are recovered.'

For the dazed bewilderment had left his eyes now, as they rested on her face.

'You—have nursed me well, Laura,' he said, with some difficulty. 'You and Tante Martha. I wanted to speak, but I could not, somehow.'

'I shall bring you some broth,' Laura said eagerly. 'Tante Martha says you must get your strength back now.'

When she came back with the broth, the old women came with her. Together they helped Stephen to a raised position, so that he could drink. It was only when he had finished, and they had gently laid him down again, that

Laura saw the strange, uncomprehending look in his eyes.

'Stephen?' she said, alarmed. 'Is your wound paining you very much?'

His dark eyes met hers.

'It does not pain me at all,' he told her, and there was dismay in his voice. 'In fact, I cannot feel anything, below the waist. I cannot move my legs at all, Laura.'

Laura felt all the colour drain from her face.

'It must be the after-effects of the wound, Stephen,' she said, not quite steadily. 'The feeling will return soon, I am certain.'

But even as she said it, her eyes met Tante Martha's, and she remembered what the old lady had said.

'You must sleep, Stephen,' Tante Martha said now, firmly. 'There is no good worrying about anything until you are stronger. Close your eyes, now, and sleep.'

Obediently, like a tired child, Stephen closed his eyes. But it was only when they were satisfied that he was indeed fast asleep that Laura followed the old woman out of the wagon.

'What is wrong with him, Tante Martha?' she asked, still keeping her voice low.

Tante Martha sighed.

'My child, when I first saw the wound, I was afraid—it seems to me that some vital part of his spine has been severed. It was a deep wound, Laura, and in such a place.'

She put her hand over Laura's, and the warm sympathy on her face was almost too much for her.

'But—but he will get better?' she asked unsteadily, knowing the truth even as she said it. 'He will walk again?'

Tante Martha shook her head.

'It is unlikely,' she said. And afterwards, Laura was grateful that she had not tried to make a pretence, grateful that she had to accept the situation from that moment.

And so, between the two women caring for Stephen, there was acceptance of the fact that he would not walk again. But they would not admit this to him, for as Tante Martha said, at that moment he needed all his strength to recover from the loss of blood. There would be time later, she said quietly, for him to accept the full meaning of what had happened.

'I suppose I shall not be well enough to ride with you when you go with Retief to settle the agreement with Dingaan?' Stephen said one day when Paul Venter was visiting him in the wagon.

For a moment, the big fair man's eyes met Laura's.

'No, I should think that is somewhat too soon,' he replied, carefully.

'Then you are going?' Stephen asked. 'In spite of your distrust for Dingaan?'

Paul Venter's blue eyes clouded.

'Perhaps because of it,' he said, after a moment. 'I know that Piet Retief has recaptured the stolen cattle, and I know that this is what Dingaan was to base the agreement on. Retief is confident—so confident that I hear he has the document prepared, ready for the king to make his mark on it, and it sets out that we are to have the land around Port Natal, and much that is beyond it.' He smiled, but the smile did not lift the cloud from his eyes, Laura saw. 'All around me, now, I hear talk that we would do better with the Zulus, and their promises of land and friendship, than we have done here, after this last attack. And—all that is true. But yet I have this inherent distrust of this man. Perhaps I can persuade Piet Retief to be a little less open in his trust. And a little less open in his talk, too. The previous time, did you not hear him, Stephen, boast of the victories of the Boers in the Northern Transvaal, over the Matabele?'

'But the Matabele are Dingaan's enemies, he would be glad to know of their defeat,' Stephen pointed out.

Paul shook his head.

'I am not so sure,' he said, slowly. 'It seemed to me, that day, that the Zulu king was alarmed that such a small band of our people had been able to defeat so many of the Matabele.'

'And is that not a good thing?' Laura put in. 'That he should realise that we are strong?'

'Perhaps,' Paul conceded. 'But this news we have now, of the Matabele being defeated at Marico, and driven north—it seems to me that it would be better that we say little of this. Although, of course, Dingaan will have heard of the routing of the Mzilikazi and his Matabele. But we should not boast of it, and I hope to prevent Piet Retief from doing this.'

He stood up.

'I ride off at first light tomorrow,' he said, and Laura knew that although he was addressing this to Stephen, he was in fact telling her. 'I hope to be proved wrong in my distrust of this Zulu Chief. And when I return, Stephen, you will no doubt be on your feet, and making plans for your wedding to Miss Conway.'

'No doubt,' Stephen agreed, cheerfully, and Laura thought that she must have imagined the momentary bleakness in his dark eyes as he held out his hand to Paul and wished him well.

At the canvas flap of the wagon, as he bent to go out, Paul turned to Laura.

'I would be grateful, Miss Conway,' he said, formally, 'if you would look after Mariette for me while I am away. Our aunt has less time now, for her husband too was wounded in the attack.'

'I shall be glad to,' Laura assured him.

'Could you perhaps walk across with me now, so that I may give you one or two instructions?' Paul said. 'In case she is ill again, particularly.'

'Go with Paul, Laura,' Stephen told her. 'If I do not rest now, Tante Martha will be in to rebuke me.'

Without a word, Laura followed Paul Venter out of the wagon, and across towards his own.

Under a tree, he stopped, and looked down at her.

'My aunt has the medicine which eases Mariette's breathing,' he said quietly. 'But that is not really what I wanted to say to you, Laura.'

In spite of all that there had been between them, her heart lifted at the way he said her name.

'If anything should happen to me,' he said, steadily, 'will you care for Mariette?'

Laura felt all the colour drain from her face.

'What do you mean, Paul?' she asked, her voice low.

He shook his head.

'I do not know,' he admitted, 'but I have this uneasiness, this feeling of heaviness.' He tried to smile. 'A strange thing, for a practical man such as I. But—will you say that you will do it, Laura?'

'Yes, I will care for Mariette,' she promised him. And then, unable to help herself, she put out one hand, 'But, Paul—'

He stopped her.

'There is nothing more to be said, Laura.' His blue eyes looked down into hers. 'How much longer before Stephen can walk?' he asked her.

'Soon,' Laura said quickly. Too quickly, she realised, for there was understanding in his eyes.

'I thought as much,' he said, slowly. 'From the moment I saw how he was wounded, I feared there was lasting damage. Does he know?'

'Not yet,' Laura told him. 'But he must, before long.'

'And you, Laura?' Paul Venter asked, his blue eyes searching her face. 'Knowing that Stephen will not walk again, do you still regard yourself as committed to him?'

She had known, deep inside herself, that he would ask this. And she had known too what her answer would be.

'More than ever,' she told him, and her voice was clear and strong.

CHAPTER
ELEVEN

'I THOUGHT as much,' Paul Venter said quietly. 'And if you had said anything else, I think I would have been disappointed, for you would not have been the Laura I have come to—know.'

Had she imagined the slight hesitation before he said the last word, Laura wondered? But it was a thought she dare not let herself dwell on.

'I wish you luck,' she said, her voice low, 'in your mission to the Zulu Chief.'

Once again Paul Venter's eyes, so blue in the brown of his face, clouded.

'I fear we may need much more than luck,' he replied. He held out his hand. 'Goodbye, Laura—I shall be gone before you rise tomorrow.'

His hand held hers for one moment, brief and warm, and then he turned and left her, without looking back. And Laura went back, then, to the wagon where Stephen lay.

Paul Venter left more than an hour before the rest of the camp rose the next morning. Laura was awake, and she heard the low murmur of voices, the restless whinnying of his horse, and then his voice in a brief farewell. She did not rise, or even look out, for she knew well that it should be nothing to her, betrothed to Stephen, that Paul Venter had ridden out this dawn to join Piet Retief and his party and go to the Zulu Chief's capital, to accept a grant of land from him. But Paul's own foreboding lay heavily upon her, and his deep unease remained with her, and in the days that followed she found it impossible to join in the plans and the dreams of the people waiting.

There would be land for everyone, people said, and green and fertile land at that. And they would be able to sleep well at nights, for Chief Dingaan's Zulus were friendly towards them. Even the English settlers at Port Natal would be glad to see them, it seemed.

Laura saw that Stephen joined little in the talk of the future, and of the plans for farming. They had begun, now, to ask some of the men of the party to carry him down from the wagon and make a bed for him under the shade of a tree, before they left on hunting expeditions. Laura had felt certain that it was bad for him to lie the whole day in the wagon, seeing so few people in those waiting days. For the trek would not move on, now, until Paul Venter returned, with the news of the land to be granted to them. It seemed to her, and to Tante Martha, that this was a wise decision, for as Stephen lay propped against his pillows, people passing would stop and talk to him.

But when the talk turned to the land and to the farms that they hoped to build up, when there was discussion of the best crops, and how the grazing would be, Stephen was silent. And one day, Laura knew she could ignore his silence no longer.

'What did you think, Stephen,' she said to him, 'of Piet Marais' plan to concentrate on crops, if the land should be as fertile as we are told? Or do you feel we should try to build up our stock instead?'

For a moment, his dark eyes met hers, and then he turned his head on the pillow, away from her.

'I would be better able to look forward to farming

again,' he said, his voice low, 'if I could see some improvement in my condition. Laura—surely by now I should be beginning to recover from my wound, and at least making some attempt to walk? But there is still no feeling in my legs at all.'

She was glad that he had turned away, glad he could not see her face. She herself felt they should be honest with Stephen, that they should tell him that it was unlikely he would walk again. But Tante Martha felt that the time was not yet ripe for that, and when she talked of Stephen needing more time to feel strong again, before having to face up to this, Laura, with some reluctance, gave in.

'It is a hard thing he will have to accept,' the old woman had said heavily, 'and he is still weak from the wound. Give him time, child, there is no need for him to be told at the moment.'

And then, taking Laura by surprise, she had asked if this would make any difference to Laura's promise to marry Stephen.

'For it is one thing to betroth yourself to a strong and healthy young man, and it is another entirely to take as your husband a man who will never walk again,' she said. 'And few would think the worse of you, Laura, if you were to find it more than you could do.'

Laura looked down at her hands, brown from the months of trekking, with the ring that had been Stephen's mother's, the tiny ring of garnets and pearls that he had given her.

'It makes no difference to my promise to Stephen, Tante Martha,' she said steadily. 'We will marry, as soon as a predikant comes.'

The old woman's workworn hand covered hers.

'I was certain you would not let him down, Laura,' she

murmured. 'But—let us wait a little, still, before we tell him he will not walk.'

And so, because of that, when Stephen spoke to her now, Laura was glad to keep her face averted, as she reminded him again that the wound had been extremely deep, that he had lost a great deal of blood, and that he must be patient.

When she was silent, Stephen reached for her hand and took it in his.

'The one good thing, Laura,' he said, and when she turned, she saw that he was smiling, obviously determined to make an effort to be more cheerful, 'is that I have discovered that my wife-to-be is even more of a treasure than I already knew her to be. If it had not been for you and Tante Martha and your nursing of me—but I will make it all up to you, Laura, when I am well again.'

Once again Laura had to turn away, pretending to search for a thimble she had dropped, so that he would not see the sudden tears in her eyes.

There was less nursing needed now, for there was not a great deal they could do for him. Tante Martha did the greater part of the care, and Laura, in spite of the constant sadness of Stephen's condition, had to hide a smile at the old woman's firm statement that it would not be seemly for Laura to look after Stephen completely, until after they were married.

Lisbet, too, had expressed her concern, but she had come to accept that Laura had no intention of looking on what had happened to Stephen as a reason for breaking her engagement to him.

One night, when it was dark, and they were sitting together beside the fire, Lisbet said, her voice not entirely steady:

'You know, Laura, your father would have been very

proud of you. And when I think of him, I can understand how you can say this makes no difference. If your father had been wounded thus, I would gladly have spent the rest of my life caring for him, because of my love for him.'

Laura was grateful for the dim light given by the smouldering fire, for when her stepmother said that, all at once a feeling of such desolation swept over her that she could have wept. Yes, she would gladly spend the rest of her life caring for Stephen—but it was not because she loved him so deeply. She was fond of him, and indeed, since she had come to spend so much time with him, her previous affection had increased, seeing his patience and his fortitude, and his constant thought for others. She admired him and she respected him, and she would never cease to be grateful to him for his steadfast loyalty to her, when she and Paul Venter came back after the night spent in the cave. But all that did not add up to the sort of love she knew Lisbet had had for her father, and therefore her caring for Stephen would be of a different sort.

'Laura,' Lisbet said now, hesitantly, in the semi-darkness. 'Laura, now that we speak of your father—' Once again she hesitated, and then Laura heard her take a deep breath before she went on. 'Laura, Piet Marais has asked me to marry him. And I have agreed. He—he will be a good father to Dirkie, I know that, and—I am fond of him. Laura?'

Laura turned to her stepmother and put both arms around this kind and gentle women she loved.

'Then I am glad for you, Lisbet,' she said, steadily. 'And—and if Piet Marais does not object to finding himself with a grown stepdaughter as well as a small stepson, I—I will be only too grateful to look on him in that way.' And then, because Lisbet's eyes were still anxiously on her face, she went on, 'I think, you know, that my father would have liked him, and—and that he would be glad to know that a man as good and as kind will be bringing Dirkie up.'

Young Dirkie himself had no trouble accepting this idea, and was soon talking excitedly of the wedding they would have when the predikant came. Often, when Laura took her class of children in the afternoon, she would have to reprimand him for his chatter of the wedding, and of the farming he would help Father Piet to do, when he should have been doing his numbers instead.

'But it is exciting, isn't it?' he said to Mariette. And then, generously, 'You can come to our wedding, if you like, Mariette.'

'And Paul as well?' the little golden-haired girl asked eagerly. 'Could the wedding wait until Paul comes back from seeing the Zulu Chief, and then he can come to the wedding too?'

'I think it could,' Dirkie told her, after a moment's consideration. 'But will he be coming soon?'

Mariette looked at Laura, her blue eyes questioning.

'Not yet, Mariette,' Laura said steadily, for there was not yet time for Paul to have joined Retief's party, ridden to the Zulu Chief's kraal, and come back again. 'Perhaps in another week.'

And then, determinedly putting aside the memory of Paul Venter's feelings of mistrust about this promised grant of land, she turned her attention to the children again, asking them questions around the small circle, listening to their spellings, and helping them as they took turns at reading from the one reading book they had. When the lesson time was over and she had dismissed the children, she put her books together, and walked over to Stephen, who was placed near enough to watch and to listen.

'If you watch us so intently,' she said to him, lightly, as she sat down beside him, 'I shall insist on you replying to the questions as well. For instance, tomorrow you must be prepared to recite for me the seven times table.'

For once, there was no answering smile from Stephen.

'Laura,' he said, quietly, 'I think the time has come for plain speaking between you and me. This wound has so damaged my spine, something vital inside, that I am not going to walk again. Is that not so?'

In spite of what Tante Martha had said, Laura knew that the time for pretence was over. This man with the steadfast dark eyes, deserved the truth.

'We are afraid that that is so, Stephen,' she replied, her voice as steady as his own had been.

'Thank you, Laura, for being honest,' he said. For a moment, he was silent, and then he took both her hands in his. 'You understand, of course, that this changes things entirely between us. There is no question of you remaining betrothed to me. I should like you to keep the ring that was my mother's, but you could wear it on your other hand.'

Laura lifted her chin.

'And I say, Stephen, that there is no question of this changing anything at all,' she told him, clearly. 'We will be married as soon as the predikant comes—in fact, we could well have a double wedding, with Piet and Lisbet.'

Stephen shook his head.

'And what are we to live on?' he asked her. 'How can I look after a wife when I cannot walk? They talk, all of them, of the farms we will be given, in this fertile land around Port Natal. What use is land to me, Laura?'

He had released her hands, but now Laura took one of his between hers.

'We will have men working for us,' she told him. 'You have your stock, you know how to deal with crops, and you have your farming equipment. You shall give the orders, and the men who work for you shall carry them out. And—and you will teach me about farming, too, so that I can report to you.'

She had never before seen tears in his eyes, and her heart turned over with a warm affection and a pity she could not deny.

'Do you mean that, Laura?' he asked, his voice low.

She did not hesitate.

'Of course I mean it,' she told him with certainty.

Still his eyes sought hers.

'There is another thing we must discuss,' he said. 'I have seen you with the children, Laura. You must realise, that in this marriage of ours—it would not be a marriage such as others. We would not have children, Laura.'

Laura felt her cheeks grow warm.

'I had thought of that, Stephen,' she answered him, steadily, truthfully. 'And I am certain that we can have a good marriage, you and I.'

She respected this man too much to hold out any false hope of any change in his condition, for she and Tante Martha believed that there could be none. But to her surprise, when Stephen, his eyes searching her face, became convinced that she meant to go ahead and marry him, there was all at once a determination and a resolution in his face.

'Then I will prove you and Tante Martha wrong,' he said, and she looked at him, astonished. 'If you will help me, Laura, I shall work to try to regain feeling in these useless legs, and then I shall learn to walk again. Perhaps with sticks, but—I shall make these legs of mine move, Laura. You shall not spend the rest of your life with a useless cripple!'

She had never heard her gentle Stephen speak so fiercely. Tears blurred Laura's eyes, and impulsively she put her arms around him and kissed him.

'I am proud of you, Stephen,' she said, a little shakily. 'And of course I shall help you.'

And so, each morning and each afternoon, she helped him to move and to exercise his useless legs. His determination impressed her, and she thought that even if he never succeeded in moving a single muscle, it was good for him that he so much wanted to. The time spent with him, and the time spent with the children, all helped her to push to the back of her mind the knowledge that surely now Paul Venter should be coming back, with the news of the land granted to them by Dingaan.

There was something else that concerned her as well. She woke one night, uncertain what it was that had wakened her, and then, listening, she heard the sound of low weeping outside the wagon. Without pausing to think, she crept silently out, and there, huddled on the ground beside the steps, was Aletta.

'Aletta!' Laura whispered, appalled. 'Whatever is the matter?'

She could not see the girl's face, but there had been a hopelessness in the weeping that had shaken her.

The blonde girl shook Laura's arm free.

'Nothing is the matter,' she said, her voice low. 'Nothing to do with you, anyway, Laura Conway. Have you not done enough harm, with your coming here and taking Stephen from me? If it had not been for you, Stephen would not now be a cripple!'

Laura felt as if there was no breath left in her body. It was true that Stephen had been wounded while fighting beside her, but—surely it was most unjust to say that if it had not been for her, he would not have been wounded?

'Do you then weep for Stephen?' she asked, unsteadily.

In the darkness, Aletta turned away from her.

'What does it matter why I weep?' she said. 'Leave me alone, for you have done me enough harm. And do not dare to say a word of this to Lisbet, or to my mother.'

Slowly, Laura went back into the wagon, not even caring that Aletta must have seen how deeply hurt she was. Often during the next few days, she felt that she could not keep the weight of Aletta's grief to herself, for there must be something wrong, she could not believe that it was for Stephen that Aletta wept so bitterly. And yet, Tante Martha and Lisbet had enough to concern themselves with, for like everyone at the camp, they were now deeply anxious for Paul Venter's return. There was no doubt that he should have been back by now if everything had gone as he expected it to at the Zulu Chief's kraal.

The women were gathered around the fires, one afternoon, when someone called out that a rider was coming towards the camp, very fast. Laura, helping to prepare vegetables, felt her hands and her heart grow still. Paul Venter, back at last. For a moment, her eyes closed, and she murmured a prayer of thankfulness that he had been wrong, that his heavy sense of foreboding had not been justified.

But it was not Paul Venter.

It was a man they did not know, and he had ridden so fast that he could barely speak. His face was streaked with the dust of the plain, and his hands, as they closed around the small glass of brandy given to him, shook.

Everyone was there now, gathered around, for the men had already returned from the day's hunting. And as they waited for this stranger to speak, a slow, sure sense of disaster grew among them, so that they were silent, waiting.

'They are all dead!' he said at last, and he looked around at the anxious waiting faces. 'Retief, and the whole party with him. Massacred, by the Zulu Chief. Him and the seventy men with him, all killed.'

Piet Retief, and seventy men with him. And one of them Paul Venter.

'Massacred?' someone repeated, shocked. 'But what happened?'

'We heard it from the missionaries,' the man told them. 'He did not kill them. They—our men with Piet Retief—were kept waiting, on various pretexts, with talk and with bargaining, for a few days. But Dingaan was friendly, and there seemed no reason to distrust him. And then, the missionaries say, he put his mark to a treaty agreeing to let us have all the land between the Tugela and the Umzinvumbu rivers.' He paused, took another drink of the brandy, and wiped the back of his hand over his mouth before he continued. 'The next day, to show that they were friendly, he asked the Boers to leave their arms and go into the royal kraal to witness a war dance, and to have a farewell feast. In the middle of the war dance, he rose, and he said, "Kill the wizards!" And they did, every one of them.' He looked at the circle of faces, but Laura thought that he did not really see them. 'My brother was one of them,' he said then, his voice low.

Slowly, terribly, the anguish of grief rose inside Laura. But she did not weep, for she was beyond tears, and—she had no right to weep for Paul Venter.

And then, as she realised that, she thought of his sister, and she turned, knowing that she had to find the child, before—

But it was too late. Mariette stood at the edge of the group of bewildered, grief-stricken trekkers. Her small face was white, and her hands came out to Laura, blindly.

'Is it true, Laura,' she asked, piteously. 'Is Paul dead?'

Laura bent and put her arms around the small figure.

'Oh, Mariette, I am afraid so,' she said, and she held the child close to her.

The little girl began to weep, then, and so did many of the women. But the stranger who had brought the dreadful news had not finished.

'And now,' he told them urgently, 'you must move your wagons to a safer place, for the Zulus are on the rampage. The night after Retief and his party were massacred they fell on unprepared laagers, and they killed everyone. I have ridden without stopping to warn as many people as I can.'

Wearily, but determinedly, he swung himself up on to the fresh horse that had been saddled ready for him.

'There is another camp farther across the plain, for I saw the smoke of their fires—I must warn them too. And if you value your lives, you must heed my warning!'

He was gone, then, and the trekkers looked at each other, frozen with the horror of this.

And it was Stephen, lying on his mattress, unable to walk, who somehow raised himself, and rallied the stunned men.

'Listen, because we have lost our leader it does not mean we can do nothing!' he said. 'If we pack and move instantly, we could reach the high koppies, and perhaps find a hiding-place.'

'We cannot do that before dark,' a man protested.

'We must,' Stephen insisted, and somehow he managed to pull himself further up. 'For I fear that if we remain here, we are directly in the path of the Zulu warriors as they sweep across the plain.'

He is right, Laura thought, and she knew that she had to push to the back of her mind all grief for Paul Venter. There would be time for grieving later, in the secret places of her heart, but only if they could survive the slaughter of the warriors.

'Come, Mariette,' she said to the weeping child. 'You are to stay with me. I will look after you.'

As Paul asked me to, she thought, as she hurried the child towards the wagon, to prepare to flee and to hide—if there was time enough to do that.

CHAPTER
TWELVE

AFTERWARDS, Laura could not believe that in such a short time they had somehow managed to pack essential belongings into the wagons, inspan the oxen, and move towards the high ground that meant a somewhat better chance of safety than the plains.

There was much that must be left behind, and there was no way that all the stock could be moved to the koppies before nightfall. But the flocks of sheep and the herds of cattle were started on their way, the herdsmen speeding their charges on faster that they had ever moved before.

Two of the families decided they were staying. By now, they said, the Zulu attack would have burnt itself out, and there was no need to flee in such haste, leaving belongings and leaving stock. Perhaps the following day they too might pack up and join the others. Without a leader like Paul Venter, there was no one whose authority would have carried weight with them.

Laura herself was entirely convinced that danger, and perhaps death, awaited them if they did not attempt to hide. Stephen felt the same, and his inability to be of practical help frustrated and infuriated him, she could see, although he said nothing, understanding that there was not even a moment for anyone to spare to give him sympathy. Two of the trekkers carried him into the wagon, and there he had to lie, while the women, with

Piet Marais helping, frantically loaded what they could, and left what there was no time to take.

To save time, and to help these women with no men other than Stephen, Piet Marais left his own wagon, bringing only a few possessions, and drove their team for them. Without his help, Laura knew they could never have managed to be ready to leave as soon as they were, and she saw, once again, that Lisbet had found a good man.

It was fortunate indeed that they had not dropped far from the higher ground, seeking only the first agreeable place to camp, while they waited for the grant of land that Piet Retief had been so certain would come. Thus, by hard driving, and by going on even when it was dusk, they managed to leave the plain behind, and to reach the koppies and seek some shelter.

'There is no point,' Stephen said, when the small party gathered in the low foothills as night was falling, 'in setting up a laager. We heard that even a laager would provide no safety for us against such hordes as these. It seems to me that we must draw each wagon back towards the trees, and although it will not be possible to hide them, at least they will not be as directly visible as if they were all together. And—if we are too late, we must not stay with the wagons, those who can must hide, in the trees, among the rocks—anywhere.'

Those who can. But he would not be able to hide, Laura thought. And all at once, now the frantic busyness of the past few hours was over, the fear that there had not been time for before, began to make itself felt.

'Laura,' Mariette said, quietly, 'are the men going to come and kill us, the men who killed Paul?'

Laura was almost grateful to be recalled from her own thoughts. She hugged the child.

'Not if we can help it, Mariette,' she said steadily. 'Come now, you and Dirkie can help, we are going to help Oom Piet to draw the wagon over there—not far, you see, but the ground is too uneven for the oxen, so we must all help.'

They lit lanterns, although they knew it might have been better not to. As soon as the wagons were drawn back, the lanterns were put out, and the weary trekkers could do no more. None of the adults slept that night, and few of the children. The herdsmen with the sheep and the cattle had not reached them before dark. They were out on the plain, at the mercy of wild animals, as well as at the mercy of the Zulu attackers who might even now be sweeping over the plain in their battle formation, called impis. They would not dare to protect themselves and their animals by lighting fires, and they must be huddled close together, men and animals, terrified.

Sometime between midnight and dawn, they heard sounds from far across the plain, and they saw many pinpricks of light. A little later, in the stillness of the night, they heard shouting and screaming—but whether of attackers or of victims, they could not tell.

When the first light came, the trekkers stretched, wearily, and looked around at each other. They were all still stunned and shocked, as well as exhausted, but they were alive, and the advancing Zulu hordes had swept on without knowing that yet another small party of trekkers was hidden here.

No one dared to move, until it was full light. Some of the men had climbed higher, to survey as far as they could, to see if it was safe to light fires, and to make some food, for there had been no thought of food the night before.

Stephen, from his mattress, now outside the wagon again and part of the circle of people, took command, a little to Laura's surprise. He seemed to see what needed to be done, and he seemed to grasp what could safely be attempted, better than some of the older men. Laura, through a daze of weariness and a depth of grief that she dared not let herself think of, was proud of him.

'We need to find out if the sheep and the cattle are safe, and if so, to bring them here,' he said. 'And we need to send a few men riding back to where we were camped, to find out if the others are safe, to lead them here, and to bring anything of value that we had to leave behind in our haste. But beyond that, I think it is best that we stay here, and remain as much out of sight as possible. For although it seems that the Zulus have swept on beyond here, there is no telling whether they may have left some warriors behind, to search for any trekkers who escaped.'

By midday, the terrified herdsmen had reached them, all but two, who with the sheep in their charge, had become separated from the others. Nothing had been seen of them that morning, but the weary watchers on the foothills saw many flocks of vultures circling in the distance.

It was evening before the three men who had ridden back to the old camp returned, and their faces told the grim news even before they spoke.

'All dead—both families,' Piet Marais said quietly. 'And—there is nothing left, of their wagons, or of our own possessions that is worth bringing, for what they could not take, they have smashed and broken beyond repair. We buried our friends, and we came away, for there was nothing more we could do.' He looked around. 'God has been merciful to us,' he said, his voice low, 'we have been spared.'

He bowed his head, then, and prayed, simply and briefly, giving thanks for their lives. And around him, each man, woman and child bowed his or her head in prayer too.

No one seemed to think it necessary to ask what they were to do now. For the moment, stunned and shocked, they all seemed to realise that they must stay where they were, in the comparative safety of the foothills. But now there was none of the busy and noisy activity there had been each day around the camp, for all hope and direction had been taken from them.

Occasionally, someone would speak, bitterly, of the massacre of Piet Retief and his party, and of the treachery of the Zulu Chief Dingaan, who had promised them land, and instead had murdered them. Laura could not listen, when they spoke thus. It was a dreadful, dreadful thing, that seventy and more men had been murdered so treacherously, but—to her shame—her grief could encompass no more than one man. With her head, she mourned the murder and the loss of the others, but with her heart and her body, she grieved for Paul Venter.

Over and over, she saw him as he had been when he said farewell to her. He held my hand, for that brief moment, she reminded herself, and his eyes looked down into mine. And then he walked away, and the sunlight shone on the fairness of his hair.

And the other times, each moment locked in her heart, all that she would ever have, now. That first sight of him, with his hat pushed back on his head, and a lazy smile as he looked at her bare brown feet when she sat on the back of the wagon. The time he dropped her in the river. The many times he stood, with little Mariette in his arms, bringing her for her lessons. And—in the cave, when he had held her in his arms, when his lips had been warm on hers.

Now that he was dead, there was no deceiving herself about her feelings for him. She had loved this man, she had loved him deeply and fiercely, and she knew, beyond all doubt, that she would never love another man as she had loved Paul Venter.

But her love for him, like her tears for him, would from now on be locked inside her heart. She would speak of him to no one, she decided, and from now on she would think only of marrying Stephen, of devoting her life to looking after him.

Her decision to speak of Paul to no one had to be changed, she found, because of Mariette. The little girl, bewildered and lost, wanted to speak of her brother, and after at first trying to stop her, Laura came to realise that this was how Mariette must come to terms with her loss and with her grief. And in a strange way, each time she held the sobbing child and listened to another memory of a Paul she had not known, a Paul who had cared for his small sister from the time their parents died, her love for him became ever more deeply rooted in her heart.

Each day, with ever-increasing determination, Stephen worked on trying to bring movement back to his useless legs. Laura helped him, knowing that this was what she must do, she must look forward now, she must put Paul Venter forever out of her mind, and she must do what she could for Stephen.

He began to talk of where they would settle, now that the land around Port Natal was not to be theirs. And gradually, he got the other men to put the past behind them, and to begin to look forward.

'We must head farther north,' he said one night. 'Perhaps towards Marico, where Potgieter cleared the land of the Matabele. Let us have just a little longer here, to make certain things have quietened down, and then, I think we must begin sending out our scouts once again, and we must once again trek. For we cannot stay here, in hiding, for the rest of our lives.'

Sometimes, watching him and listening to him, Laura felt very humble. He could so easily have become bitter and depressed, but instead he was in many ways more positive than the men who could walk.

'And the first thing we will do, as we move on,' he said to Laura, 'is to ask where we may find a predikant, so that we can be married.' And then, with a smile that betrayed some anxiety, 'That is, if you have not changed your mind, Laura?'

'No, Stephen,' Laura told him, steadily, 'I have not changed my mind.'

For if I did not with Paul Venter alive, she thought, I certainly will not, now that he is dead.

There was little to do during those waiting days, and once Laura began to force herself to put her thoughts behind her, she became anxious about Aletta again. The blonde girl was clearly in some state of distress, and Laura wondered that neither Lisbet nor Tante Martha seemed to see. Again, more than once, Laura heard her weep during the night, but remembering what Aletta had said before, she lay silent, waiting for the younger girl to come back into the wagon.

And then, one night, she could bear it no longer, and she crept out after Aletta. It was moonlight, and she found the other girl very easily, crouched under a tree, once again weeping.

'Aletta,' she said, her voice low, but determined. 'There is something wrong, and you cannot go on keeping it to yourself like this.'

Aletta raised her head, and Laura could see the tearstains on her face. For a moment, Laura thought she was once again to turn away, and then, as if making up her mind, she flung back her blonde head.

'You are right,' she said shakily, 'I cannot go on keeping it to myself for much longer, for it is the sort of thing that will not be kept.'

For a moment, Laura looked at her, not understanding, and then, slowly, she realised what Aletta meant.

'You mean, you are—pregnant?' she asked, with some awkwardness.

'Yes,' Aletta replied, brusquely. 'Now you know why I am weeping.'

Laura tried to recover from the unexpectedness of this.

'It is not the end of the world, Aletta,' she said, after a moment. 'Babies have been born out of wedlock before this.'

'I know that,' Aletta replied. 'But—this is more difficult.'

'Could you not marry, even if the time would be short?' Laura asked.

'I doubt that,' the younger girl said, bleakly. 'For the man who is the father is dead.'

Dead? No, it was not possible that she could mean Paul.

Laura did not know she had said his name aloud, until Aletta repeated it, and there was something almost triumphant in her eyes.

'Paul?' Aletta repeated. 'So it bothers you, Laura, to think that Paul Venter fathered my child?'

Laura, sick with shock and hurt, turned away.

'It is nothing to me,' she said, knowing the other girl was not in any way taken in. 'It—it is more to the point, what you are to do now.'

'If he had lived, of course we would have been married,' Aletta murmured, and Laura knew that she was watching to see how Laura would take this.

'Of course,' she agreed, and somehow she managed to lift her head high. 'Had he—was there talk of marriage between you?'

The moment she had said it, she wished she had kept silent. For Aletta looked back at her, and in the moonlight there was a spiteful pleasure in her eyes that made the hurt even deeper.

'But of course,' she replied. 'If there had not been, would I be carrying his child?'

Laura turned away.

'I know nothing about what you would have been doing,' she said.

'Nor about Paul Venter,' Aletta flashed back. 'For I see it surprises you, this news of mine.'

Yes, it surprises me, Laura thought, with a sudden weariness of spirit, but why should it? There was nothing between Paul Venter and me that should make me feel I had any right to know anything of any importance about him. And, there was that night, she remembered now, when she had looked across in the firelight, and seen him with Aletta.

'Tante Martha will have to know soon,' she said, quietly. 'And Lisbet.'

Suddenly, violently, Aletta's hands caught hers.

'You are to promise not to tell them,' she whispered, fiercely. 'Promise me, Laura.'

'Why should I promise you anything?' Laura retorted,

and she pulled her wrist back, rubbing it. But even as she said it, she knew that she could not be the one to tell her stepmother, and the old woman she had become so fond of. 'But I will say nothing, Aletta. Until you do—and surely that must be before long.'

'You can leave that to me,' Aletta said. And then, as suddenly as it had come, her anger was gone, and she smiled at Laura. 'Just as I leave you with the thought that I am carrying Paul Venter's child!'

Laura stood up, and walked back to the wagon, unable to take the taunting on Aletta's face any longer. For there was no doubt that however bad the other girl's problems were, she was finding pleasure in Laura's distress.

It is nothing to me, she told herself again and again, in the next few days. But it was of little use to say that, when she knew all too well that this had hurt her deeply. In some ways, she thought painfully, this was harder than learning to accept Paul's death. How could he, she thought, desolate, have spoken to me as he did, just before he left? How could he have taken my hand in his, how could he have looked down at me when he said farewell?

And before that, in the cave. No, that thought was more than could be borne. I will never again think of that night, Laura told herself passionately. And from now on, this is Aletta's problem, I will have nothing more to do with it.

But a week later, she had no choice but to become involved in the younger girl's problem, for Aletta, bending over her in the wagon in the night, woke her.

'Laura—please help me,' she said, and Laura could hear the terror in her voice. 'I'm ill.'

She turned then, and went out of the wagon. Laura

hesitated, but only for a moment, knowing she could not ignore the plea that had been in Aletta's voice. Outside, she followed Aletta from the clearing where the wagon was, and reached her just as the younger girl collapsed.

The night was clear, and soon it was all too evident to Laura, although she had known nothing like this before, what was happening to Aletta. She did what she could for the girl, and afterwards, when it was all over, she went to the stream for water to clean her. It was only when Aletta leaned back against a rock, white and exhausted, that Laura thought of something.

'Aletta,' she said, quietly. 'Did you—take something, so that this would happen?'

'No,' Aletta replied quickly. Too quickly. And then, without opening her eyes, 'Yes, I got some herbs from old Sanne, one of the coloured servants. But—I never thought it would be like this. Oh Laura—now that it is over, now that there is nothing to worry about, promise you will never say anything!'

Laura looked down at her.

'I have no wish to tell anyone, ever,' she said, and she made no attempt to hide her contempt. 'Now, it is almost light. I suggest that we go back to the wagon, and we tell your mother and Lisbet that you must have eaten something that made you violently ill, and you called for me to help you. That will explain your—distress, and your pallor.'

She had to help Aletta back to the wagon, for the younger girl was obviously very weak. But there was no difficulty about their story being believed, and Laura thought, with a bitterness that was entirely new to her, there was nothing easier in the world than to deceive people who loved and trusted you.

It took only a few days before Aletta was fully recovered, and sometimes Laura, looking at her, thought that it seemed that the whole experience had hardly touched her. She herself, she knew, would never be the same again. For although she had known that what she felt for Paul Venter must be put behind her, firmly and completely, yet there had been a secret place in her heart that she had known would always belong to him.

Now that secret place had been torn from her, it was hers no longer, because of what had happened between Aletta and Paul. Even her secret memories of him could be hers no longer.

She was glad when there was talk of trekking again, when plans began to be made for them to move on. They would be a smaller party, without the families and the wagons that had been lost in the Zulu attack, and without the stock that had been lost too in that dreadful night, but slowly, surely, their optimism had returned, and now they were once again determined to move on, to find a place where they could settle and live in peace, and begin farming again.

The days began to be busy, as preparations were made for moving on. Each person had to share in the work for there was much to be done. Laura, gathering wood one day, was on the lower slopes of the foothills when she saw a horseman riding towards their small camp. It was not one of their own men, she knew, for they had all been out early, and come back.

The man had not seen her, and as the path grew steeper he dismounted, leading his horse. He looked very weary, Laura thought, with pity. Surely he must be a fugitive from a trekking party which had been attacked.

She went towards him, meaning to welcome him, and then, hearing her step, he turned.

'Hello, Laura,' he said, quietly.

Laura felt all the colour drain from her face.

It was Paul Venter.

'We thought—you were dead,' she said, unsteadily.

He shook his head.

'No,' he said, and the exhaustion in his voice tore at her heart. 'No, I am not dead.'

She took one step towards him, both hands out, and then she remembered Aletta.

CHAPTER
THIRTEEN

'LAURA?' he said again, and now there was a question in his voice, as he saw her draw back.

She shook her head, unable to trust her voice.

'It's all right,' he said then, and the gentleness in his voice would have unnerved her completely, had she not remembered Aletta, carrying his child and losing it. 'I have not come back thinking to change anything, I know and I respect your promise to Stephen.'

He took a step towards her.

'No!' Laura said, more loudly and more violently than she had meant to. But even if she had not made a promise to Aletta, she could not have said anything to Paul. It had happened, and because of it, nothing was the same. She turned away. 'I shall fetch someone, you must be exhausted,' she said, hardly knowing what she was saying, wanting only to get away from him.

But at that moment, two of the men, having heard her call out, came through the trees. They stopped at the sight of Paul, and after a moment called out his name, obviously hardly able to believe their eyes. After that, there was so much calling and activity, and other people appearing, that Laura was able to slip away. She wanted to find Mariette, and tell her, quietly, about her brother. The child had been so well recently—Laura herself thought that the higher ground agreed with her—but she was still frail, and to have a shock like this, on top of all she had been through—

Mariette was with Dirkie, helping him to pack one of the kists under Lisbet's supervision. Already in the distance Laura could hear the excited greetings, as more people realised that Paul Venter was here, and alive.

'Mariette,' Laura said, and she knelt beside the child. 'I have some wonderful news for you.' Even to say his name was not easy, but it had to be done. 'I cannot tell you how it has happened, but—Paul is not dead, after all. He is alive, and he is here. Look—there he comes, through the trees.'

The little girl looked at her, and all the colour drained from her face. And then, following Laura's pointing finger, she turned, slowly.

'It is Paul,' she whispered. 'It is.'

At the other side of the clearing, the big fair man stopped, seeing the child. And Laura, looking at him in spite of herself, saw that he had not expected to find his beloved little sister here, and well. For a moment, they both stood still, the big man, and the golden-haired child, and then they ran towards each other, and Paul lifted Mariette right off her feet, into his arms.

All around, there was the buzz of excited talk, speculation as to what had happened, but now Tante Martha stepped forward.

'You can see, surely, that he is worn out,' she said severely. 'Piet, take him to the stream and let him wash, and then he must eat, and he must drink. We can wait until then, to hear his story.'

An hour later, when they gathered round the fire, waiting for Paul to finish drinking the hot sweet coffee, Laura saw that he looked much better now. But there were lines of bitterness around his mouth that had never been there before.

'There is little to tell,' he said at last, quietly. 'As we were riding to Dingaan's capital, a messenger came from another trekking party to say that they, too, wished to be considered for land grants. Piet Retief asked me to change places with this man—to let him go to the kraal, while I was to ride back to his party, faster than he would be able to, for he had been riding for two days. I was to tell them what had been promised, and to stay with them until the settlement was completed.' He shrugged his shoulders. 'And it was as simple as that. I was not there when Chief Dingaan gave the order to kill, and his warriors fell on our men and massacred them. It is only now that I have been able to reach you, for the whole countryside has been in turmoil, as the impis have swept over it with their slaughter of any party of trekkers they could find.' For a moment, he closed his eyes. 'I—did not think to find my own people alive, truth to tell.'

'You were distrustful of the Zulu Chief from the start, Paul,' Stephen said after a moment. 'And how right you were.'

The grim line of Paul's mouth became even harder.

'I wish to God I had not been,' he replied, his voice low. And then, with an effort that was all too obvious, he lifted his head, and tried to smile. 'But the blackest days are over, and we must look forward. Although we have lost some of our party, there are enough of us left to go on.' He looked around, at the half-prepared wagons. 'It seems to me that you were making ready to move on.'

Eagerly, Stephen began to tell him of their thoughts of moving north, towards the part where Potgieter had beaten the Matabele, and chased them even farther northwards. Paul Venter listened, not saying anything.

'It is a good thought, Stephen,' he said at last, slowly. 'But—as I have ridden here, and made contact with surviving parties of trekkers, I find that there are many people who feel that Retief and the men who fell with him must not go unavenged. This Dingaan must be taught a lesson he will never forget.'

One of the older men shook his head.

'How could that be possible?' he asked, reasonably, 'So few of us left?'

Paul Venter's clear blue eyes gazed ahead, unseeing.

'That I do not know, yet,' he admitted. 'But it must be done.'

There was no talking among the men that night, for as dusk fell, it was obvious that the man returned from the dead was worn out. But the next morning, early, Paul Venter was up talking to the remaining men. Laura, as she helped Lisbet and Tante Martha to prepare food, heard his voice, clear and decisive, in the discussions.

It was Paul who insisted on the women being brought in on the plans to be made.

'For your lives, and your futures, are at stake as much as ours,' he said, quietly. 'As I see it, we have two choices. We can head north as we are, a small party, leaving behind us all that has happened, and hoping only for some land we can call our own, somewhere. Or—we can head farther into the foothills of the Drakensberg, and we can join with other parties of trekkers who have survived and, when we are all together, we can reach some decision about settling our score with this murderer, before we seek to settle. And it is not only the thought of settling our score that makes me say that —vengeance is one part of it, but the other is that we would wish to see this land safe, and these savage Zulus tamed. Now, what say you, Tante Martha?'

The old woman folded her hands together and looked at the big fair young man. Her eyes were steady.

'When a person is old,' she said, after a moment, 'the thought of peace is pleasant. But it seems to me that I could not dare to ask for peace, with the memory of these murdered men. I say we join the other trekkers.'

And that seemed to be the feeling of the whole party. Even Stephen, who had been keen to head north, agreed that in the long term, this was the best plan.

To join with the others who had survived the slaughter, they would have to go down again on to the plains and head farther north, before climbing back into the foothills again. So, the following day, they began to do this, reaching the plain comparatively quickly, and falling easily into the way of trekking once again.

But this time, Laura thought, with love and with pity, Stephen was not one of the young men riding out ahead to find the way for them, or to hunt for the day's food. Instead, he lay in the wagon, uncomplaining and cheerful, and each day, when they made camp and he was carried out of the wagon, he would concentrate, with complete determination, on the exercises he was working on, to make his legs move.

'I will do it, Laura,' he told her more than once. 'These legs will move.'

'I believe you, Stephen,' Laura replied, and somehow, in spite of what Tante Martha and the other women said, his determination had convinced her.

They talked, the two of them, quietly, about the possibility of finding a predikant among the trekkers gathered together. Stephen said that he had asked Paul, and Paul felt certain there would be one. But Laura did not wish to have Paul Venter's name in this discussion, and if it had been possible not to have thought of him or mentioned him at all, she would have been glad, she told herself often.

Yet, in spite of that, she could not help noticing him when he was near her. He was so many different things, this man, she sometimes thought. With little Mariette he was gentle and loving, and sometimes, watching his blue eyes rest on his small sister, Laura could hardly believe that at another time his lean brown face would be grim and bitter, as he talked of making the Zulu Chief regret what he had done to the trusting trekkers in his kraal.

The one thing that she could not help noticing, was that he made no attempt to talk to Aletta, or to go near her, as far as she could see. In the circumstances, this did indeed seem strange, and at last Laura decided that this only proved how despicable he was, for he seemed neither to know nor to care that Aletta might have been with child.

And so much, she thought, with a satisfaction that made her immediately ashamed of herself, for Aletta and her talk of marriage. For it was all too obvious that Paul Venter certainly did not have marriage on his mind or in his plans!

More than once, he tried to talk to her, and made an attempt to thank her for what she had done for Mariette. But each time Laura barely let him start, before she brushed him off, and moved away. And then, one late afternoon, when the oxen were outspanned and the camp was preparing for the evening meal, he came on her as she was gathering wood, some little distance from the camp.

'No,' he said quietly, determinedly, when he saw that she would have hurried past him. His hand came down on her arm, hard. 'No, Laura, this time you will let me speak. I know you feel that it is better that we do not have anything to do with one another, and I respect and admire your decision to stay with Stephen. But you must allow me to thank you for what you did for Mariette, for the way you comforted her and helped her to accept my death. She has told me, and—I can never thank you enough, Laura.'

Laura, with nothing but Aletta in her mind, lifted her head and looked at Paul.

'I do not want or need your thanks,' she said, and once again she tried to draw away.

He would not let her go.

'I promise you, Laura,' he said, quietly, 'that I will never do or say anything that would cause Stephen concern. But because you are to marry him, does not mean you have to hate me, surely?'

A wave of anger swept through Laura.

'It is not because of Stephen that I wish to have nothing to do with you,' she said unsteadily. 'It is because of Aletta.'

'Aletta?' he repeated, and the astonishment in his voice, the bewilderment in his eyes, confirmed her contempt for him in his lack of concern for what had been between Aletta and him.

'Yes, Aletta,' she flung back at him. 'It is obviously nothing to you that she carried and lost your child, that she might have died herself, that she—'

She stopped.

There was a still, growing anger in Paul Venter's face that suddenly frightened her.

'What are you saying?' he asked her.

Falteringly now, she repeated it. He listened, his eyes on her face as she spoke. When she had finished, he was silent for a moment.

'Wait here,' he told her brusquely, and he strode back

towards the camp. Laura, knowing that she should have taken the chance to go, could do nothing but lean against a tree, trembling, her eyes closed, feeling she might faint if she were to move.

In no time at all, it seemed, he was back. She opened her eyes, to see him striding back towards her, pulling Aletta by the hand, until the two girls were face to face.

'Now,' he said, coldly, 'I want the truth of this. Aletta, I have told you what Laura said. What is your explanation? Because you know, and I know, that if you did indeed carry a child, it certainly was not mine.'

Under the contempt of his blue eyes, Aletta's blonde head bent.

'I did not actually say it was yours,' she said, her voice low. But this was more than Laura could take.

'But you did,' she told the other girl, shakily. 'You know that you did.'

Now Aletta lifted her head.

'I said that the father of my child was dead,' she reminded Laura. 'It was you who immediately thought of Paul Venter. And—when you said his name, it seemed to me best that I should agree.'

Paul's eyes met Laura's.

'Do you mean,' he said, slowly, 'that you immediately thought of me when you knew that she was pregnant?'

Laura could not look away.

'I thought of you,' she said with difficulty, 'only because when she said the father was dead, I—could think at that time of the death of no one but you.'

She turned to Aletta.

'And you let me think it,' she accused the other girl. 'You—you even told me there had been talk of marriage between you and Paul.'

Aletta shrugged.

'I had to name the father,' she said, her voice cool now. 'And we all thought Paul was dead, so—it seemed to me that his name would do.'

Paul swung round, looking down at her.

'And whose name was I covering for?' he asked, his voice icy.

Aletta hesitated, but only for a moment.

'It matters not at all now,' she said. 'For there is nothing more to worry about. He was Jacob du Toit, and he remained with his wife and his children, in the wagon down on the plains, in the path of the Zulus.'

'A married man,' Paul said.

'A dead man, now,' Aletta returned. And then, re-covering herself somewhat, she looked at Laura. 'But it is all over now, and if you should ever think to make any accusations, I would deny everything.' Without either of them making any attempt to stop her, she walked away.

'Let her go,' Paul said, when Laura at last moved. 'She has done enough harm.'

He was silent for so long that Laura knew she had to speak.

'Paul,' she said unsteadily, 'you must understand, it was not that I thought that you—it was just that when I heard that you were dead, I could not seem to think of any other man being dead, only you.'

'It is almost worth everything that has happened, Laura, to hear you say that,' Paul murmured. And then, his voice as unsteady as her own, 'Oh, my love, that you should go through all this time thinking that of me, that you should have to doubt, even for a moment, that you are the one love of my life. Laura, Laura.'

He held her close to him, and he kissed her hair, her forehead, her cheeks, and then her lips, gently at first, and then not at all gently. Then, when she could barely stand, he held her back from him, and looked at her.

'You are crying,' he said, with wonder, and gently he wiped the tears from her cheeks. 'No more tears for me, Laura, you must promise me that. And—I will promise you that this will never happen again. This is all that there will be between you and me. Soon you will marry your Stephen, and I—I shall be a hunter, and a fighter, and perhaps later a farmer, and often, when I am an old man, I shall tell myself that long ago, I held Laura in my arms.' He had finished drying her tears, and now he pushed her from him, gently. 'Now go, Laura, back to Stephen.'

Slowly, as if in a dream, Laura walked back towards the clearing where the wagons were. She never knew, afterwards, what she said to Lisbet or to Tante Martha or to Stephen during that evening, but as early as possible, she pleaded a headache, and went to bed. But not to sleep, for she lay awake for most of the night, thinking of what Paul had said, thinking of the way he had looked at her. And in the morning, she knew that it would be all right. She would go on with her life as she had planned, she would marry Stephen, she would help him to walk again, and to farm. And no one would know, ever, that there was a secret corner of her heart that would always belong to Paul Venter.

Somehow, in some way she could not really understand, she knew that it was going to be easier to go on, now that she knew that there was no truth in what Aletta had made her think about Paul. Somehow the cleansing of this bitterness, the returning to her of this tiny part of her that was Paul's, had made the future easier.

In the next few days, as they slowly made their way nearer to the foothills of the Drakensberg, where the other surviving trekkers were gathered, Laura found that she could speak positively and certainly to Stephen about their marriage, about the farm they would one day have.

'We shall indeed have that double wedding,' she told Lisbet. 'For it is more than time you and Piet should marry.'

'I think so too,' Dirkie agreed. 'Father Piet is going to teach me to shoot, you know, Laura.'

For one moment, there was an ache in Laura's heart when she thought of how her own father would have loved to see this small son of his growing up, to have himself taught him to shoot. But Piet Marais would be a good father to Dirkie, she knew that.

A few days before they would reach the other trekkers, there were disquieting rumours of bands of Zulus in the area, and they began, once again, to set up laagers each night, protecting the spaces between with thornbushes, and having someone always on watch. The men and women of the party began to sleep lightly, and to start at the slightest sound.

And then, one night just after midnight, it happened. Suddenly the laager was surrounded, and the guns, always ready, were brought out and into action, firing instantly in defence of their small party. Piet Marais fired from one end of the wagon, and Stephen, dragged quickly into position and propped there, as they had planned earlier in the day, from the other. Lisbet loaded for Piet, and Laura for Stephen. And Laura, in the midst of the fear and the frantic and constant re-loading, was proud of Stephen, for he must have been uncomfortable and possibly in pain, but his only concern was to keep firing, to keep defending their laager.

Afterwards, she could never be certain how it hap-

pened, for it was so swift. Suddenly, incredibly, one of
the huge black Zulus was there, through the barrier, his
assegai raised above Laura. In the same instant, Stephen
moved—*moved*, Laura realised only afterwards—the
assegai struck, and Piet Marais shot the Zulu.

There was no lessening in the ferocity of the attack,
but Laura, with no thought for anyone but Stephen,
knelt down beside him, hardly conscious of Tante
Martha taking the gun, and going to fire from Stephen's
position, with little Dirkie loading for her.

'Stephen,' Laura said, tears streaming down her face.
'Oh, Stephen!'

When he spoke, she had to bend close to him, to hear
what he was saying.

'You see, Laura, I did move, didn't I? I knew I could,'
he murmured.

'Yes, Stephen, you moved, and—you saved my life,'
Laura said unsteadily.

For a moment he looked up at her, and he smiled.
And then, quietly, in the midst of the battle raging
around them, he died, in her arms.

CHAPTER
FOURTEEN

ALL through the night, the little band of trekkers fought
to defend their laager against the attacking Zulus.

Laura, when she realised that she could do no more
for Stephen, laid his head down gently, and then took
back her place at the gun from Tante Martha. On and
on, in the hours of darkness, the defenders fought, firing
only when they could be certain of hitting, for their
greatest problem now was the lack of ammunition.

Somehow, they could not help feeling that if only they
could last out the night, there might be a chance. And in
the first light of dawn, they were proved right in this, for
suddenly the waves of attacking savages ceased. There
was a brief lull, and then the defenders, hardly daring to
believe it, saw that the Zulus were retreating. And
there, galloping from the foothills, was a band of trekkers, coming to their rescue.

'We are saved,' Lisbet said to Laura and her mother.
'For we could not have lasted much longer.'

They all knew that, but it was only now, when they
were safe, that the full horror of that knowledge could be
grasped. So it had been with Stephen's death. It had
happened, and they had known it, but there had been no
time to think of it, no time to dwell on it, no time, even,
to weep for him.

Until now.

Laura looked at the peaceful face of this man who had

loved her so steadfastly, who had in the end given his life for her, and she wept. For Tante Martha, he had been the son she had never had, and for Lisbet the young cousin she had grown up with, and so the three women wept together. Young Dirkie wept a little too, for he had been fond of Stephen, but as children will, he recovered soon, and went willingly with Piet Marais to see the trekkers who had come to their rescue.

They buried Stephen that morning, under a lonely tree. There was nothing to mark his grave, but he would not be forgotten by the people who had known him and loved him, Laura knew, as she stood at the side of the quickly-made grave, and listened to Paul Venter read a few verses from the Bible, and say a few words about Stephen Smit, his courage, and his unfailing spirit.

When it was done, he came over to where Laura stood beside Tante Martha.

'I am sorry, Laura,' he said, his voice low. 'He was a brave man.'

'Thank you,' Laura murmured, and now her tears were over, but there was an aching tightness in her throat that made it impossible for her to say anything more.

As soon as possible they set off, now under the protection of the men who had come to their aid, for the foothills of the Drakensberg. There they found other parties of trekkers encamped. Every few days, more arrived, until they began to look like the old united laager they had had at Graaff-Reinet.

The certainty grew, among those who had survived the Zulu attacks, that there would be no peace, and no chance of the settled life they had come so far to find, unless the Zulu Chief Dingaan was defeated. A commando was formed to attack Dingaan, and Paul Venter and Piet Marais rode off. But the commando was defeated, and the leader, Piet Uys, was killed. For a time after that, there was no further talk of sending out forces against Dingaan. Laura, who had seen her stepmother's face, white and anxious, as she waited to see whether Piet Marais would come back, was glad of this, but she knew this was not the end of it.

Lisbet and Piet Marais were married soon after that, quietly. Laura could remember when Lisbet and her father had been married, but somehow, over these long months, she had at last come to accept her father's death, and she could feel only happiness for this quiet, gentle woman who was the only mother she could remember.

Tante Martha had somehow managed to arrange a small party, and the people who had trekked with them joined them in celebrating the marriage. Laura could not help thinking, throughout the day, that if Stephen had lived, they would have been married now as well. And she was glad to work hard, glad to have little time to think of this.

She was making coffee when Paul Venter came to lift the heavy kettle for her.

'Thank you,' she said, 'but I—I can manage.'

He took the kettle from her, and set it back on the fire.

'You are working too hard, Laura,' he told her. 'You have hardly stopped today, and ever since we came here you have kept yourself busy. You are too thin, and you hardly sit down—and you contrive, always, to move away when I come near you.'

Laura felt her cheeks grow warm.

'Laura,' Paul said, gently, and he took both her hands in his, 'Stephen would not wish you to spend the rest of your life mourning for him.'

Laura drew her hands away from his.

'I'm sorry, Paul,' she said, distressed. 'I know I owe you more than this, but it's too soon.'

He looked down at her, and there was a cold anger on his face that began to penetrate the wall that she knew was between them.

'Don't ever talk to me of owing me anything, Laura,' he said curtly. 'I want nothing of that sort from you.'

Laura had not meant it in the way he had taken it, but somehow the effort of trying to make him understand was too much for her. She watched as he walked away from her, and she could do nothing to put this right between them.

The weeks, and then the months, passed. The trekkers began to build huts, to plough, and to sow. There was news that Andries Pretorius, a farmer from Graaff-Reinet, was organising a large trek to come to their aid.

Laura spent most of her time with Tante Martha, now that Lisbet was married to Piet Marais, and with the children. Her small class had increased, for there were many men and women who were only too glad to have their children taught to read and to write and to learn their numbers. But always, when the school-time was over, it was little Mariette, Paul's small sister, who lingered with Laura, to help her, to talk to her. And Laura found herself growing as close to the child as she was to her own small brother.

The clear, pure air in the foothills seemed to agree with Mariette much more than the air of the plains had, and although she would never be a robust child, there was at last a little colour in her cheeks.

'You have done wonders with that child, Laura,'

Tante Martha said one day when Mariette had just gone.

Laura shook her head.

'The air agrees with her, that is all,' she replied.

But the old woman would not agree.

'It is you, and your interest in her, that has made the difference,' she said firmly. 'And her brother thinks so as well, for he and I were talking about it the other day.'

Laura said nothing, but she bent over the kist to put her books away.

'Laura,' Tante Martha said, quietly. 'I have said nothing, for you needed time, but now I must speak. Stephen would not have wished you to go on this long, mourning for him. Come, sit down beside me, child.'

Slowly, Laura closed the kist, and sat down beside the old woman.

'You must not feel bad, Laura, because you did not love Stephen as much as he loved you,' Tante Martha said. The unexpectedness of hearing her deepest concern put into words made Laura give a small, revealing gasp. Tante Martha put her workworn hand over Laura's. 'You were loyal to him, Laura, and because of that, Stephen died a happy man. Yes, child, I mean that. He died in your arms, secure in your affection for him, and happy because he had been able to move, and he had saved your life. Laura, you remember the peace on his face. Could you deny that he died a happy man?'

Laura looked into the once-bright eyes, filled now with love and kindess.

'I—had not thought of it like that,' she admitted, with difficulty. And for the first time, she could allow herself to realise that she had been feeling guilty about Stephen.

'Then think of it like that now,' Tante Martha told her

briskly. 'And, when you have thought, go and tell Paul Venter.'

Once again Laura could not hide her astonishment. Or her panic.

'I could not do that,' she murmured, distressed. 'We —we parted with some hard words on his part.'

'I know that,' the old woman replied placidly. 'Yes, he needed someone to talk to, your Paul.'

'He—is not my Paul,' Laura said, her voice low.

'He will not be, unless you take the first step,' Tante Martha agreed. 'Laura, child, what does pride matter when you love someone?'

Laura thought about that, throughout that day. And she thought, too, of what Tante Martha had said about Stephen. And slowly, certainly, she came to see that it was, indeed, as simple as Tante Martha had made it seem.

When it was dusk, and the camp-fires were glowing in the growing darkness of the sky, she went to Paul. She had been watching him as he talked to some of the other men, and when he walked away from them and sat down on a fallen tree, she followed him.

'Paul,' she said, softly.

He looked up. For one moment, the blazing joy in his eyes told her all she wanted to know, and then it was gone, and his face was closed.

'Did you want something?' he asked her, coolly.

He was not going to make this easy for her, Laura knew, but she would not give up now.

'Yes,' she told him, clearly, firmly. 'I want to tell you that I have been very foolish, and—and—'

Her voice faltered.

Paul Venter stood up then, and looked down at her.

'And what, Laura?' he asked, very quietly.

All at once it was not too hard to say, for Tante Martha was right, what did pride matter, when you loved someone?

'I love you, Paul,' she said, with complete certainty.

For a long time, it seemed to her, he stood very still, looking down at her, his eyes searching her upturned face. And then, slowly, he smiled.

'Laura, Laura girl,' he murmured, 'you have kept me waiting so long.'

And with no thought for anyone who might be near, he took her in his arms and crushed her to him, his lips hard on hers.

'I think,' he said at last, not quite steadily, 'that we must be married before too long. What do you think, my English girl?'

'I think so too,' Laura agreed. She looked up at him and smiled. 'Yes, I think so, my Boer trekker.'

But her Boer trekker, she found, was not prepared to marry her before he had been part of the force that was to mete out justice and revenge to the Zulu Chief.

'Why not, Paul?' Laura asked him. 'We could be married now—and the combined commando will not go out before Pretorius reaches here.'

Paul shook his head.

'I will not leave you a widow, Laura,' he told her. 'And—I will not marry you until I know that this land is safe for you and I and the children we will have.'

There was no moving him from that, although others did not feel the same way. In October, Aletta married Louis Malan, a young farmer she had met since the remaining trekkers joined together. Laura was sincerely glad for Aletta, but she could not help wondering if this restless, unhappy girl would really find contentment now. For the sake of the young farmer, she hoped so.

There were other marriages, too, but Paul remained firm. His first concern was to do what he could to make this land safe for them and for their children.

In November, Andries Pretorius came, and he brought a cannon with him. Immediately, preparations were made for the commando that would attack Dingaan and his Zulus, and before the end of November, Paul Venter kissed Laura goodbye, and rode off with the other men.

A little way off, he turned. His hat was pushed back on his sunbronzed head, and he waved to her. Laura, through her tears, managed to smile, and to wave back to him, although Mariette, beside her, would not look.

'He will come back to us, Mariette,' Laura told the child, with a confidence that she had not known she possessed until that moment.

In the middle of December, news was brought to them that the force of five hundred grim and determined men, had crossed the Tugela, and were riding towards the Zulu Chief's capital at Umgungundhlovu.

'They held a church service on Sunday the 9th,' the scout told the anxiously-waiting women and children, 'and Sarel Cilliers made a vow, that if God gave them victory, the trekkers would build a church, as a memorial, and would for ever after remember that day.'

Soon after that, they heard that victory had indeed been given to the trekkers. Wave after wave of the Zulus had been driven back by the fire of the Boers, and finally the trekkers had counter-attacked, and had driven off their enemy. They had, indeed, killed so many that the river was already being called Blood River.

It was not long after that before the commando rode back to the camp, weary, exhausted, begrimed from the dust as they rode. But quietly triumphant, and satisfied that although Dingaan still lived, he would not again harry them as he had before.

Men had been killed, but as Laura had known, in some strange way, not Paul Venter. He swung himself off his horse, and he took her in his arms and held her close. For that moment without passion, but with the peace of a man coming home.

They were married a week later, with only those who knew them well in attendance. Mariette was allowed to wear her prettiest dress, and to call herself their bridesmaid. And Dirkie, full of importance, helped his mother and his stepfather and his grandmother, to act as hosts.

'This is my new grand-daughter,' Tante Martha said, for Mariette was to move to the sky blue wagon, now much faded and in some need of repair, to keep her company, she said. Laura knew, with love and with gratitude, it was to allow Paul and her to be alone.

And that night, as she lay in his arms, she knew that this was indeed the love she had dreamed of, the passion and the tenderness she had longed for. Paul was in turn demanding and tender, passionate and gentle, and Laura knew that each moment since they met had been leading to this wonderful and never to be forgotten consummating of their marriage, in the wagon that would be their home, until they finally found a place to put down their roots.

The next day, the men began making the necessary repairs on the wagons, for although many of the trekkers had decided to stay where they were, Paul, and Piet Marais, and some of the other men, had taken a decision to head for the newly-established settlement called Pietermaritzburg. There, they felt, they would have the advantages of the settlement near them, but enough land for everyone who wished to farm.

Paul lifted Laura up and sat her on the seat at the front of their wagon the morning they were to leave. Behind them, the other women were ready in their wagons, and the men on horseback beside them. What remained to them of their sheep and their cattle, were herded beside them.

'Soon,' Paul promised, looking up at Laura, 'we will have our home. Can you bear it, Laura, to trek again?'

'I think I could trek for the rest of my life, as long as we were together,' Laura told him, meaning it.

He laughed, and pushed his hat back on his head.

'I shall not ask you to do that, love,' he told her.

He rode off ahead, seeking out once more the way of the wagons. And slowly, surely, the line of wagons set off once again, following. Laura, her hands brown and strong on the reins that controlled the oxen, felt her heart lift as the sun rose, and they began to head for their new home, wherever it might be.

How to join in a whole new world of romance

It's very easy to subscribe to the Mills & Boon Reader Service. As a regular reader, you can enjoy a whole range of special benefits. Bargain offers. Big cash savings. Your own free Reader Service newsletter, packed with knitting patterns, recipes, competitions, and exclusive book offers.

We send you the very latest titles each month, postage and packing free – no hidden extra charges. There's absolutely no commitment – you receive books for only as long as you want.

We'll send you details. Simply send the coupon – or drop us a line for details about the Mills & Boon Reader Service Subscription Scheme.

Post to: Mills & Boon Reader Service, P.O. Box 236, Thornton Road, Croydon, Surrey CR9 3RU, England.
*Please note: READERS IN SOUTH AFRICA please write to: Mills & Boon Ltd., P.O. Box 1872, Johannesburg 2000, S. Africa.